Man's Best Friend

By Ahmed Salah

ISBN 978-1-9991704-0-0

Table of Contents

Preface

Desirous though I am to speedily begin my story, I feel I'd be remiss if I didn't start by preempting what I'm sure will be a common criticism of it: that it's an attempt to present myself in a more favorable light than I deserve. This suspicion doesn't stem from any assumptions regarding the cynicism of my readers, as I know readers to be the most thoughtful of people, but rather, the knowledge that as pathetic as such a mischaracterization of oneself may be, it is not beneath me.

You see, it was clear from the onset of writing that given the nature of this book, any distortions would defeat its purpose, so I was able to keep myself from knowingly making them. But during the process of emotional inventory, which writing necessitated, I was forced to confront a tendency—I assume subconscious in nature—to reframe events, almost in real time, in such a way that I'd be able to live with myself. This is true for everyone at least to some degree, as evidenced by the shock we've all felt upon realizing we actually weren't the object of someone special's desires—but, for one in possession of their mental faculties, as I assume you are, these delusions are eventually detected and uprooted, however painful that may be.

In my case, however, because of a vulnerability present throughout my life—which serves to amplify the anguish inherent in the recognition and eradication of delusions—the preservation of my sense of self-worth seemed to override all else, resulting in periods of egoic detachment from reality. Extensive psychiatric treatment has enabled me to better recognize and rectify these derailments, but I cannot be certain a few of my delusions haven't passed unnoticed into this book. As such, I felt it prudent to begin with this clarification rather than risk being thought a liar.

Counteracting this failing of mine required the adoption of an earnestness that, depending on your moral outlook and your exposure to the workings of a mind ordered such as mine, might give you cause to pass judgment upon me. Understand that though many of the thoughts, and sadly, even actions of mine that are outlined in this book are depraved, their depravity is now clear to me, and my inclusion of them is not meant to justify or even glorify them. It is due only to the necessity of equipping the reader with all the information necessary to attribute to me whatever theory of mind they so wish.

Far be it from me to tell you to not condemn me or even to wait to the end to do so, but I venture to ask that, if you do feel a rising revulsion within yourself, you keep it at bay long enough to understand my contextualization, and if you do choose to chastise me after that, I ask further that it is tempered with an understanding of how difficult all this was for me to admit.

Benign Douchebaggery

My epiphanic realization, for which this chapter is titled, occurred in the lead-up to the anniversary dinner for my now ex-girlfriend's parents. We treated them to a celebratory dinner each of the five years we'd been dating, and it would have been a routine event had it not been for the significance I'd built around it in the preceding weeks. I'd been going over our time together, prompted by a vague listlessness, and soon convinced myself both that I should propose marriage and that the dinner would be the perfect setting to do so. The decision to time it thusly wasn't romantic—I knew that because of her childish romanticism, she'd be so sentimental that acceptance was almost guaranteed—but neither were my motivations, which, to elucidate, I will treat briefly on our relationship.

We'd met outside a lecture in the first week of university as I stood alone, watching my classmates pairing up, ruing my neglect of orientation week's bond-forming function and my resultant decision to forgo it. The fear that consumed me, that my loneliness was a preview of my university experience, had put such a damper on my libido that I'd have taken no notice of her, beautiful though she was, had it not been for the terror I noticed in the faces of every guy she would look at. Gaining her approval, I felt, would demonstrate that I was not subject to the gynophobia that so consumed my classmates and would serve as a good first step toward building a reputation for myself. My seduction proved successful, and within weeks I was recognized as the guy with a hot girl, a circumstance which—at least in this milieu—vested me with an aura of reverence. I didn't think my motivations all that shallow or uncommon, in large part because I could see that her feelings toward me were as egotistical as mine (my pursuit meant her worthy of interest); however, I began to question whether they were foundations for a stable bond.

After the wooing phase was over, we gradually settled into what she must have thought was an equilibrium, which, despite eliminating the quarreling that had been occurring with increasing frequency—as we reconciled our ideas about each other and relationships with reality—made me uneasy. Instead of entering into a healthier dynamic, what occurred was that by learning to control my eye rolling, faking excitement, hiding my disdain toward her friends, etc., I became better at managing her expectations that—because of the natural disillusionment that comes with being in a long-term relationship, as well as my persistent undermining of her romantic ideals—were dwindling. All of this meant that, taxing as it was to me, our life together was all that she could hope for. What fanned this into a mild resentment on my part was the sense that the work of maintaining our relationship was entirely mine, a burden that grew as it became apparent that commensurate effort would not be made on her part. My continuing status as her boyfriend, the knowledge that I was making her happy, and sex—that diminished both in frequency and intensity over time—were to be my only rewards.

This not only changed my relationship with her but also my encounters with other women, who benefited in their juxtaposition with her because of the relative absence of stress during our interactions and the potential I'd feel with each of them, however short-lived it was. My girlfriend was, in turn, helped by a disillusionment of my own, caused by my increasingly lackluster experiences with other women, that what we had, dissatisfying though it felt, was all we could reasonably expect. Her increasing entrenchment into my life—I grew less and less able to think of it unfolding without her—meant that, despite my dalliances, I never seriously considered leaving her. Even the knowledge that she'd never forgive me for having cheated on her and that any continuation of our relationship would be based on the lie that I had been faithful wasn't enough to keep me from a proposal of marriage. So, I purchased a ring and prepared for the dinner, all the while scanning my reasoning for any faults.

As the night approached, however, I began to worry that because of the early disintegration of my own parents' marriage, I didn't have enough of an understanding of what marriage was to commit myself to it. A half decade spent in at least partial contact with her parents could have made up for this deficit, but since I was sure, from the night I first made their acquaintance, that gaining their approval was all but a certainty—both of them seeming amenable to ego stroking—I never considered them worth thinking about. Now, however, convinced that my girlfriend must have construed her conception of relationships around the dynamic she witnessed growing up, I felt that their lives offered the best insight into my own marital future. I resolved to take her father out before the anniversary dinner and extract insight.

He suggested we meet, sot that he is, at a bar near his house, which a cursory glance at a review website indicated was a dive. I knew there was no way I could wear any of my usual clothes to such a place without making both him and the other patrons feel inadequate, so I rummaged through boxes in search of anything casual I might have kept from my college years. My search drew the attention of my girlfriend, whose offer of help I accepted before I realized that in going through my closet, she might discover the ring.

The need to come up with an excuse before she invited herself inside the closet prevented me from processing my shock, but once I'd convinced her that I must have donated them and made my way to a thrift shop to purchase something as trashy as her father, I wondered if that shock wasn't all the proof I needed that this marriage would be wrong-headed. If the prospect of being unwittingly precipitated into an engagement was so dreadful as to be physically jarring, might that not mean my consideration of marriage was based in part on a degree of self-delusion only recognizable subconsciously? Was that reaction an innate drive to flee from pain that I, to some extent, anticipated? Once the adrenaline died down, though, I was able to see that it wasn't a rare, let alone unprecedented feeling for me; it was more likely a result of sensing a plan I'd invested in slipping away, not some sort of prescience. If I kept the ring with me at all times, I thought, there'd be no need to change course.

Washing the clothes twice before leaving for the bar meant I arrived later than expected, a circumstance I feared would give her father enough time to get incoherently drunk, rendering the night pointless. But he must have been unsure whether I'd cover any drinks he had polished off before I got there, and I saw him sipping on what was probably his first glass of water in days. My plan entailed waiting until his first mention of his wife, then coaxing him into describing crucial junctures of their relationship beginning with their meeting, hoping that by imagining myself in those situations, I'd be able to discern his reasoning. It soon became clear, however, that due to vast generational, cultural, and most importantly, intellectual gaps I imagined to exist between us, my scheme wouldn't work. I'd have been worried, were I not so confused by the way he related the story of their wooing.

I assumed he was taking the same braggadocious tone that had always been his default, because despite a few mentions of his wife's lost beauty and waning affability, he only ever seemed to describe the fixtures of his life when he met her—his hair, his muscle car, his medals, etc. But he was too transported in the retelling to give that quick, childishly insecure glance he'd always follow his boasts with to see if his interlocutor was impressed. Instead, it seemed as if the validation of these status symbols by his wife— inherent in her acceptance of his marriage proposal— had reinforced his pride enough that even though the things underpinning it are now all gone, he is still able to lose himself in it. Pitiful though it was to see a grown man reminiscing in such a way, I almost felt happy for him because I knew that his reverie was an improvement over his pathetic life.

His excitement didn't diminish as he relayed the discovery of the pregnancy, the resultant shotgun marriage, and their purchase of a new home. But then he trailed off. I could only assume that he'd come back to the present since he was watching a game and pedantically rattling off baseball trivia. I didn't take offense to his abrupt shift to the television, since I could tell that his focus on the game was clearly an attempt to hide a paroxysm of sadness that came over him, and in hindsight, I'm surprised I managed to fake interest in his commentary well enough to avoid offending him, since I was so caught up trying to understand the sudden jump from excitement to misery. The difficulty of juggling the task of putting on a display of attentiveness and gleaning his emotional state was probably why I wasn't able to keep track of my drinks as well as I would have liked.

Something made the gulf between his conceptualization of his younger self and his present reality apparent to him, but what was it? It had to have been a memory, since he was trapped in them at the time, but nothing in his story seemed to have been the trigger. His mention of an office job struck me as odd since I'd been told he'd always been working odd jobs, so when the game went to commercial, I asked him what it was like. He reddened, but thankfully, when he began talking, it became apparent that his anger was with the situation and not with me.

He explained that his wife felt his income insufficient to expand their family and had been trying to convince him to seek a raise. He resisted at first, since he knew his boss to be miserly, but his wife launched a campaign of alternating degradation and flattery that was so effective that she convinced him both that he was so essential his demands had to be accepted, and that he wasn't worth shit if he couldn't get the raise. Thus inflamed, he asked for an audience with the boss. In his fervor, he failed to account for the fact that the business was being transferred to the boss's son, who was, therefore, at his side at all times. If he had, he'd have realized that their meeting would be used as a case study in hardball labor negotiations.

He attempted to back out once he registered, for the first time in their working relationship, enmity toward him from his boss, assuming him to be in a bad mood, but he was told that important matters had already been pushed back for him, and he wouldn't get another meeting. Though the respect he showed to both father and son—he addressed them as "sirs" despite the boss's curtness—bespoke an impressive level of restraint, it wasn't enough to sway the two men, and, after feigning consideration, the boss gave him a flat *No*. His dredged-up rage, especially when relaying the son's thinly veiled amusement at his humiliation, was such that I had to gesture to a concerned waitress to reassure her we'd be fine. Most shocking to me was that instead of reacting to his story with either my usual bemused contempt or even simple pity, I felt only indignation, as if it were happening to me. Unfamiliar to me though this sensation was, I felt confident in labelling it empathy, and since my seeming inability to feel it was often angrily mentioned to me during arguments, frequently alongside an amateur diagnosis of sociopathy, I thought I'd take this opportunity to explore this emotion and its implications.

Afraid of the way his wife would react if he gave up on the matter so easily, he pleaded his case again, citing his years in the boss's employ, as he knew him to be a man who valued his loyalty. This seemed to resonate with the boss, but after the son whispered something into the boss's ear, he refused again, saying—presumably in the hopes of ending their increasingly tense encounter—that it would be unfair to the son to make such a commitment just before handing over the reins, and that it would have to be his son's decision once he took over.

He went on to explain that, knowing that this hand-off was only a few weeks away, he desisted, and instead embarked on a charm offensive directed at the son. He'd bring him coffee, compliment him on his suits, and give him little tips about the business, like the tricks his coworkers used to get out of work. Although all this made him feel like a rat, he convinced himself it would be worth it; however, his kowtowing only managed to annoy the son, and as soon as the handoff took place, he fired him.

I slammed the table, knocking over our drinks, but fortunately he'd built enough of a rapport with the staff over the years that we weren't asked to leave. I excused myself to dry off and to cool down, but as soon as my mind drifted away from him and toward my own emotional agitation, I noticed the return of my anxieties regarding the proposal and tried to remind myself I had more important things to think about. It was baffling to me that the contemplation of the life of one so pitiful could have wiped such pressing concerns from my mind, and I spent so much time attempting to understand this stress-relieving aspect of empathy that her father had to come into the restroom to check on me.

Cognizant as I now am of the cascade of benefits this little shift in thought would come to have on my life, I find myself fighting the tendency to provide an overly rosy account; in actuality, I was switching between a sense of crestfallen pity for this sad, old drunk and rage at his treatment. Only by having some familiarity with the ennui and existential angst that had come to define my intellectual existence could a person have detected the subtle transformation in thinking brought on by this emotional propinquity with another human being. It wasn't the difference between feeling good and feeling bad; it was the difference between feeling a wide range of emotions and being devoid of all but perturbation and intermittent shots of pride.

There are those who are blessed with a vapidity that ensures them a life of uninterrupted bliss. When faced with a problem like my uncertainty regarding the proposal, they readily convince themselves to accept any notion that cheers them up. On them, the significance of my emotional discovery will be lost; but for those of you who, like me, are too perceptive not to notice life's capriciousness, too enlightened not to notice its general banality, and too courageous not to confront these realities and are, by virtue of your intellect, set—as if on train tracks—toward a life of depression, only you, my miserable brethren, will know how excited I was to find that all of this could be broken out of simply through fellow-feeling. Of course, the use of empathy solely as a means of pulling one's self away from unwanted trains of thought is douchey, but it is, I think you'll admit, a more benign douchebaggery than I'd hitherto embraced.

Once we got back to the table, which by that time had two plastic cups of beer atop it, he took a more paternal tone with me, warning me that my anger would get me in trouble one day. I worried that I had alarmed him and had lost the approval I had taken for granted, but in actuality, he had merely recognized within me the same impulse that he said had "ruined my life."

I was repulsed at first that such a man could think of me as a younger version of himself, but then he explained to me that the violent daydreams I'd just been having—of savagely beating that prickish son—was what he actually did upon being fired. I tried to convince myself that I'd have had enough foresight to realize I'd be opening myself up to prosecution, jail time, and the life of a convicted felon and would have avoided it all, unlike him, but I knew that I couldn't have made any such guarantees. Then I remembered the calming effect of my epiphany, and I desired to see if empathy could be used as a tool to control similar impulses.

The pang of disgust I'd just had when he likened me to himself, however—the polar opposite of the way I wished to train myself to react—was a sign that the maturity I desired wouldn't come from one realization alone, and that I'd have to reorder my thinking so that this lesson was foremost in my mind, especially when stressors, like this comparison, worked to push me toward old modes of thinking. I had to admit to myself that even if this man was as pathetic and as beneath comparison to me as I initially felt, the contemplation of his emotions was a superior alternative to my normal thoughts. My superciliousness, comforting though it had always been to me, was preventing a genuine emotional connection, and therefore had to go.

This was both a sad indictment of my somewhat narcissistic tendencies of thought, and more importantly, a lodestar against which the course of my life could be realigned. I swore to myself then and there that I'd put my restroom contemplations into action and work toward being more empathetic, if only for the relative serenity I might gain. Even though my current subject's miserable life and lack of admirable traits made this a relatively poor time to test out this line of thinking, I was wise enough to channel that revulsion into motivation to empathize with someone less pitiable—that is to say, anyone else.

The thought of marriage, of course, was thrown out the window, as working my way to an indefatigable capacity for empathy took top priority, and the manipulation of an entire family to attain it seemed to run contrary to this more important goal. As I attempted, somewhat hypocritically, to chart my course, my philosophizing was interrupted by his laughter; he noticed I hadn't followed a joke and repeated himself: "I said the plant was automated the next year. I would have been out of a job anyway." I laughed along, but as I attempted to regain my train of thought, my hypocrisy of ignoring someone to think about how to be compassionate dawned on me, and I decided that I'd be better off listening to him in earnest as practice.

He turned the conversation back to his wife, and his bitterness re-emerged. He blamed "the bitch" for having coerced him into challenging his boss into giving him a raise. While his rude reference to his wife upset my modern sensibilities to a degree—I've always considered myself a moderate feminist—when I reexamined his actions under the assumption that we were more or less alike, I realized that it was an animosity not dissimilar to—although older and more intense than—what I had felt toward his daughter on numerous occasions. Such contempt toward one's partner, I assumed, would inevitably define any relationship that one enters to reinforce their egoic conceits, which was invariably the case for both me and my girlfriend. Either we'd have to reimagine our relationship, which—assuming she was even capable of doing so—would probably entail a lengthy break, or we'd have to separate altogether, both of which, I knew, would cause her anguish.

I tried to think of any way to soften the blow, but my emotions got the better of me, and my interlocutor noticed my eyes welling up. I attributed my tears to allergies and excused myself once again, but I'd drank more since my last trip to the restroom, and in my haste, I fell getting out of my chair. I tried to lift myself up immediately in hopes of staving off what would have been embarrassing attempts by the father to assist me, but I didn't realize until I rose that no assistance had been forthcoming, as he was transfixed on the ring box that had fallen out of my pocket and spilled its contents onto the floor.

He picked up the ring with one hand; then, weeping, he embraced me, which caused quite a bit of consternation among the other regulars at the bar. I suspect they thought he was accepting a proposal I'd made to him, and because of their homophobia and self-flattery, were imagining whether their previous interactions with him had been subtle attempts at seduction. The bouncer had made his way over by the time the confusion was cleared up, and disturbed by the degree of my inebriation, kicked us out. My girlfriend's father offered me a ride, which I refused, citing concern over his drunk driving history; instead, he called me a cab. I couldn't bring myself to tell him I'd made a mistake buying the ring, and all I could muster was a request that he not ruin the surprise.

The mature course of action seemed clear—to provide her with a full explanation of the misunderstanding and of my altered emotional trajectory—but through my cowardice or feelings of distress, that pathway seemed closed off to me. Instead, I took to devising a plausible lie, but the taxi arrived at our apartment before I could complete the task, and I was left with no choice but to ask the driver to wait while I planned an escape.

Luckily for me, upon opening the front door, I heard the sound of our shower, which I hoped meant I'd have enough time to get in and out without detection. But I only managed to pack some boxers and undershirts before her ringtone started emanating from the bathroom. I froze, unsure whether I should focus on packing clothing that could be worn to work or run for my life; however, hearing the shower turn off followed by a "Hi, Dad!" sealed the deal. I hightailed it to the door and managed to get there simultaneously to a gleeful shriek, which served to drown out the sound of me exiting the apartment.

I repeatedly mashed the elevator call button, so desperate was I to get away; but before it arrived, I heard another shriek, brought on this time, I assumed, by the discovery of my ransacked closet. I ran to the stairwell door, going through and gently closing it just before she stuck her head out our front door to scan the hallway. I stood, breathless, as she called my name with an increasingly quavering voice until—the tears finally getting the better of her—she wailed and slammed the door, at which point I ran, coward that I am, downstairs to the safety of the cab. The alarm on my cabbie's face I took to mean he thought he was an unwitting accomplice to a robbery, so to put him at ease, I tried my best to explain, but I was cut off by a phone call from her.

I tried to calm her down but was cut off by her invectives on the subject of my penis length, which were so loud that they were audible to the cabbie, who tried but failed to stifle his laughter. Matters weren't helped when she confused his laughter for mine, and to teach me a lesson, she swore to destroy anything and everything that I had left. In an attempt to deescalate the tension, I told her we'd talk again and hung up.

After regaining his composure, the cabbie apologized profusely and offered to give me a discount if I wouldn't complain to his employer, but nothing could have been further from my mind. The knowledge that this commotion, though cataclysmic in my life, was in his but a pleasant diversion, was such a psychic balm that any fury or embarrassment I had melted away. Not only did I feel beneficent for having given this man what assuredly was a respite from his mundane life, but I thought that if in his perusal of my life for comic fodder, he empathized— even inadvertently—I could be even more pleased with myself for the added gift I'd bestowed upon him.

Learning to detach from angst with empathy in the restroom seemed to make life bearable, but the thought that I could impart this on others gave my life meaning, so much so that I devoted myself to evangelizing the gospel of benign douchebaggery. Looking back at it all now, it's clear that it was the thrill that I felt at the prospect of a life peppered with moments like these that kept me from falling apart entirely during what would be a rather raucous emotional journey.

Disillusion

I began to suspect during the cab ride—and became certain upon arrival at the home of my now former friend—that the task of communicating my newfound bliss to others would be more difficult than I had imagined. If, as Arthur C. Clark said, "Any sufficiently advanced technology is indistinguishable from magic," I suppose it would make sense that any sufficiently advanced worldview would be indistinguishable from schizophrenia, and thus, I cannot blame my friends for their confusion. But the frustration and alienation, both minor at first, grew with each failed attempt at explanation, and soon, proving my sanity became my sole focus.

Now, I don't want to give you the impression that I broke with my friends because they couldn't understand me, as that would genuinely have been nuts. Habituated as I am to first seeking fault within myself before attributing blame to others, I assumed that I was merely incoherent; however, even though I quickly became able to articulate it as clearly as I did in the previous chapter, my attempts to rephrase only managed to make them worry about my mental health. It was then that I began my consequential exploration into the possibility that the barrier to their understanding did not lie with me.

The rift between my stated desire to increase the general stock of happiness and my seeming inconsideration of the depression my departure had set my ex into was all anyone dwelt on, and I found myself unable to come out from under the accusations of hypocrisy. I was patient at first, as I assumed their concern to be genuine, and I even felt quite a bit of anguish under the weight of their chastisements, but that waned when they proved themselves uninterested in helping me reconcile this dissonance, and instead, only wanted to convince me to give up what I'd learned. For them, the immediate repercussions of my epiphany were enough to dismiss it without taking the time for consideration, and any emotional dividends, either forthcoming or presently apparent, possibly because of my aforementioned difficulty with communication, were dismissed as fantastical.

I felt I should have expected such a reaction, since it was only natural that I'd have gravitated toward people with the same values as mine, and this new sense of morality must have been as alien to them as it would have been to me just a few days prior. So instead of giving up on them then and there, I attempted to coax them down the road I'd traveled. The most obvious person to start with was the friend who, in addition to being closest to me emotionally, was the closest to me geographically, as he'd allowed me to cohabitate with him. He was eager to take me in because he had a lot of free space after his wife moved out. I tried to get him to see how his thinking contributed to the disintegration of his marriage, and I urged him to rectify his mistakes before separation came to divorce, but my attempts only invoked anger, the kind of statements like "Mind your own fucking business, you lunatic!" which he would levy at me whenever I'd try to enlighten him. I took this anger to mean I was striking a chord and that further inquiries would get more traction, but all they got me was an eviction.

Things weren't much better at work, as I'd lost the favor of my managing director, who'd noticed the evaporation of my drive for self-advancement and the resultant lack of concern for his unspoken rules, the most important of which was that no one was to arrive later than him. It wasn't my fault—I'd just been in such a reflective mood that I lost track of time in the shower—but he dismissed this as a lie, saying that our meeting was called partially to discuss complaints about my body odor. I wouldn't have believed it had it not been corroborated by my erstwhile roommate, but apparently, my shower philosophizing sessions had been so stimulating that I'd forgotten to apply soap. Insulting as this was, before my epiphany I probably would have begged his forgiveness and promised to change course, but I decided instead to share my gift with him.

Here was a man whose role at the firm—an enforcer of rules that exist solely to pad its bottom line—formed the entirety of his self-conception; occupying a social position so unnatural for a human would necessarily have a deadening effect on his basic decency, as he'd be disconnected with humanity as a whole. Although this was evident to everyone who worked under him, because of the increasing attention he'd put into and pleasure he'd take out of torturing his underlings, it didn't yet seem evident to him. So I apprised him of it.

I told him that he could mitigate his alienation, and maybe even re-tether himself to his fellow man, by taking the time to engage on a more human level with the people in his life—certainly at work, but primarily at home. Cognizant as I was of his wife's desire, expressed two drinks into every office party, for more sexual attention, I recommended that he might try coming to work a few minutes later himself and spend the extra time with her, killing two birds with one stone. Although I failed to enlighten him, I managed, at least, to bestow another gift of laughter—this time to the security guards he called to escort me out of the building.

Untethered to the city and unburdened by, rather than bereft of, both employment and friendship, I was free to relocate to a place more suited to quiet contemplation: my childhood home. Though vacant since my grandmother's death two years ago, the house had seen little attention since my father's death half a decade earlier, which meant I'd have to do quite a bit of maintenance, but I thought of it as a pleasant diversion from my near-constant introspection. Though that proved to be the case, I quickly yearned for some human contact and decided to meet my neighbors.

Armed with a bottle of wine I found while cleaning the cellar, I went next door, but even though the lights were on and I could hear the barking of a dog, there was no answer. I knocked again, and though I listened to the dog running to the door and scratching it from within, there was still no sign of a person—that is, until I heard a second set of footsteps approaching, and the dog went silent. Certain that the owner of the house was looking at me through the peephole, I smiled and said hello, but instead of hearing the door unlocking as I'd expected, I heard only the diminishing sound of the dog's whimpers, as if it were being dragged from the door. I stayed put, thinking that the dog was just rambunctious, and the neighbor was putting it away out of courtesy, but after a minute or so of standing around like an idiot, I went home, thoroughly embarrassed, and drank the wine myself.

I was too busy cursing my most unneighborly of neighbors to generate any insights during that first bottle, but the second, although it did nothing to mitigate my anger, weakened my focus enough that my passion was more diffused, and I reasoned that the problem wasn't with the neighbor, but with the society in which such treatment of one's neighbors was considered normal. I thought about moving to a place less fragmented, but although I found many such locales, it seemed that their unity was borne out of a dependency on one another that is the result of the relative harshness of life there, not some innate enlightenment; I found myself unwilling to subject myself to those conditions. I chastised myself for my weakness, but doing so was not nearly as painful as realizing how far away from my goal this weakness meant I was. I already knew the path to enlightenment would be long, but I was uncertain of its length, all too aware of its difficulty, and unsure whether I'd be able to make. It appeared as though my neighbor, whom I'd been heaping calumnies upon, was a better person than I, for they were merely ignorant of their deficit, whereas I was actively shunning the cure.

I tore myself apart, thinking alternatively of my cowardice and baseness, until upon noticing tears welling in my eyes, I was forced to confront the fact that such a minor snub could send me into a tailspin. Although I was still convinced of the superiority of my new mode of thinking, I felt this spoke to a relative disadvantage: that people now had power over my emotional state. Thinking about others is impossible without, at least at times, thinking about their immorality, which was, in turn, impossible without confronting one's own. By the time I'd finished the third bottle, misanthropy and depression had taken hold of me, and I was tempted to forgo my journey altogether, assuming I was better off as a jaded, self-absorbed prick.

Desperate not to accept these conclusions, I tried to push them out of my mind, hoping to reevaluate my situation in the morning, but unable to sleep, I spent the night fighting back visions of a destitute, lonely, anguish-filled future. I left bed convinced I'd destroyed a perfectly good life and dedicated myself to rebuilding it. I thought it prudent to liberate a few more bottles of that delightful wine, both for the trip back and as tokens of apology for alienating everyone I knew, but as I removed a stack of my father's old books from a box with the intention of repurposing it as a bottle holder, I stumbled upon his copy of *The Divine Comedy*, and remembering his assertion that the book did more for him than any of the psychiatrists he'd consulted, I thought it wouldn't hurt to read the first Canto, if only to avoid any nagging regret at not having done so.

Although this Canto is mostly remembered for the beautiful description of the feeling of depression it opens with, as Dante comes to himself inside of the forest, what moved me was the fear that compelled Dante to re-enter it once his path was blocked by the three beasts, most notably the wolf: "As one who, with his gain elated, sees the time when all unawares is gone, he inwardly mourns with heart-griping anguish; such was I, haunted by that fell beast, never at peace, who, coming o'er against me by degrees, impell'd me to where the sun in silence rests."

Literary scholars still debate the symbolism of the beasts, but I won't waste your time trying to interpret the intentions of a dead man who, like the scholars, was possibly crazy himself. What mattered to me was that the beasts made the forest inviting by comparison, as my recent anguish had made my previous life. Convinced that in order to have put it so aptly he must have felt it, and knowing, from the book's structure, that he had eventually overcome it, I vowed to read the book until I'd discerned how.

I realized very quickly that my first pitfall was trying to go down this spiritual path all alone; in fairness to me, I had assumed I was forced to do that by the closed-mindedness of my friends, but I should have sought guidance. Therapy being off the table, as it would have been tantamount to admitting to the others that they were right about my mental state, I set about following Dante, as he, in turn, followed the poet Virgil.

Inferno was the most helpful; its structure, transitioning through increasingly horrific circles of hell, each dedicated to a fountainhead of human depravity, allows one to gradually inure oneself to thinking along these lines, which is necessary if one is to attain my goal of indefatigable happiness. One begins by reading, imagining, and digesting Dante's *Inferno,* but one inevitably also creates and populates their own.

Although this begins as an angry process, in my case reliving the slights done upon me by such varying people as my former friends, my old managing director, and most recently, my neighbor, thinking about what cardinal sins belie their grotesque actions and assigning them to their circle, there will be times where an honest reader will find themselves guilty of the same intransigence that they damn others for; it forces one to remember things they took great pains to forget and assess our reasoning before committing regrettable actions. This recognition of one's own capacity for shittiness and gradual realignment of one's worldview necessarily has a cooling effect on one's thoughts regarding human foibles. Having gone through a few iterations of this with each of my major hatreds and failings, the agitation I felt about interacting with people in my new vulnerable state dissipated, and I began to feel ready to re-enter society and put into practice the lessons I had learned in the bar's restroom.

My first trip out of the house, three days after being sent reeling by my neighbor's affront, although partially a test of my emotional durability, was primarily a quest for more wine, my dad's collection having already been exhausted. Despite a certain level of fear I couldn't shake, I was quite optimistic; there was also an inkling of pride, as I was pleased with myself for having had the patience and the courage to not give up on humanity. No sooner had I loaded my shopping cart, however, than my resolve began to wane.

The cashier seemed to expect that a man in my condition—I hadn't showered, shaved, or brushed my teeth since I'd moved—would pay for his drinks with panhandled quarters, so my presentation of a premium credit card took her by surprise. She asked to see a piece of ID, worried, I assumed, that I was underage, and flattered, I told her I was old enough, but she repeated her request, saying that she wouldn't allow me to use the credit card unless I furnished ID. Shocked by her superficiality though I was, I forgave her for it, and rather than giving her the stern lecture on making assumptions that I initially felt she deserved, I simply apprised her of my credit card company's merchant agreement, which did not require her to see my ID, and assured her that she wouldn't get in any trouble for going through with this transaction. She refused again, thinking that calling me *sir* would be enough of a veil for her growing contempt.

I desperately tried to quell the anger rising within me until I noticed that her haughtiness had given way to fear, and I felt returning to me a sense of social control that, until its evaporation during this interaction, I'd taken for granted; here, though, that control was borne out of fear of my potential violence, not fear of my status. Thankfully, before I could unleash my fury on her, I was startled by a "Dude, what the fuck?" from the gentleman behind me in line. My anger waned when, shifting my focus onto him, I remembered he had done nothing wrong, and that—already the victim of a senseless delay caused by this despicable cashier—he stood to have his suffering exacerbated if I created more of a commotion. Out of consideration to him, I provided the cashier with my ID.

She held it up to compare the photograph thereon with my face for what couldn't have possibly been enough time to determine anything, then returned it, saying it wasn't me in the picture, and demanding I leave. Flummoxed, I searched for words to reason with her, which only made her threaten to call the police if I didn't go immediately. Being spoken to in this manner, as well as the prospect of going without wine, so enraged me that, despite my hatred of such vile language, I found myself screaming, "Listen, you—" but before I could add the pejorative, which I see no point in transcribing, the gentleman behind me, to whom I had just shown kindness, presumably thinking he was reciprocating it, whispered that I shouldn't embarrass myself. Knowing myself to be suffering an indignity is one thing, but having it blamed on me, especially by one I'd expected to take my side, was too much.

The cashier must have noticed me reaching for a bottle—even I hadn't noticed it myself until she shrieked—and she warned the customer I was going to hit him with it. I was aghast at my reaction, but the man's adoption of a fighting stance, the cashier's repeated screams for help, and her characterizations of my mental health so enraged me that I now found myself tempted to smash the bottle on the counter and stab them both. I didn't, but only because the wail of a little girl, piercing through the cacophony of screaming, shouting, and gasping from the other customers, snapped me out of my frenzy.

She was running toward my would-be combatant, her arms extended as if she were trying to grab hold of his leg; when she was restrained by a woman who, though silent, was herself wracked with fear, I immediately knew them to be the man's family. The thought of how close I came to destroying their lives by murdering him in front of them brought on such a pointed feeling of disgust that the bottle fell out of my hand; I fervently apologized, but the man, probably wanting to end the altercation before I reached for another bottle, attempted to grab me, and there was nothing left for me to do but run, crying, out of the liquor store.

I was forced to confront the advantages, both for myself and others, of my former emotional detachment; the relative stability of my self-absorption I noted after my neighbor's slight came back to mind, but added to it—because of my horror at the depth of my anger—was a concern that I'd harm someone in a similar fit of anger. For a person as sensitive as I am, to whom even such minor provocations could elicit a nearly murderous rage, aloofness seemed almost adaptive; it's hard to imagine how high the bodies would have been stacked otherwise. There was nothing to do but to return to my old life, but I thought it'd be fitting if first, I returned to the liquor store after cleaning up; I didn't want to fight the cashier, only to go through with the purchase, and point out her superficiality to her before complaining to her manager.

These angry meditations made me run home faster, so eager was I to freshen up, then put her in her place, but when I ran out of breath and slowed to a walk, my anger seemed to lose momentum along with me—I was probably too oxygen-deprived to maintain the level of cognition necessary to keep my fury on life support—and by the time I'd rested, my thoughts were replaced with yet more self-chastisement over my wretchedness. I was particularly horrified at the lengths to which I'd go to preserve the deference I'd grown accustomed to—first violence, then the withdrawal of her means of sustenance by getting her fired—and my self-disgust manifested in tears; I sobbed the rest of the way home.

Had I been stopped on my way by a religious leader, a psychiatrist, or even a two-bit life coach, I'd probably have begged them for guidance and dumped the task of piecing myself together on them; fortunately or unfortunately, people were either too awed or afraid to come anywhere near me. For the most part, the onlookers would turn away upon my noticing their stares, usually to laugh to themselves, or remark to their buddies, but there were those who maintained eye contact, either to make me aware of their contempt and the superiority over me it implied, or—rarely—to take pity on me. Drawn as I was to that last cohort, they'd prove more disgusted by me than any of the rest once I approached; I felt I couldn't blame them, as their only problem with me was that they were good enough judges of character to recognize a reprobate, and I started running again.

By the time I reached my neighborhood, the streaming snot from uncontrolled crying and the cardiovascular strain from running combined to make breathing so hard I'd have collapsed if it hadn't been for the jolt I'd get whenever I noticed another gawker. I was so distraught that it was only when I'd made it halfway up my porch stairs that I saw, sitting in front of my door, a wolf. My thoughts vanished, replaced by that passage of Dante, and I stared at the beast, horrified, not so much at its presence as at the fact that this hallucination proved my detractors right: I was nuts. I cried until, noticing it inching toward me, I scampered backward and tumbled down the steps, hitting my head on the pavement.

I forced myself up with the intention of running away, but, when I looked at the creature again, I saw that it wasn't a wolf, but just a husky; I could only lie back and laugh as waves of relief rolled over me, but soon the dog was atop me, and I froze. This wasn't out of a sense of fear, but rather from wonderment, because staring into its eyes, I noticed—as I had in the bar's restroom on that night with my ex's father—the absence of everything I'd been worrying about. It began licking me, and although I was too consumed with giggling to think too deeply on anything, I couldn't shake the feeling that maybe, this husky was my Virgil.

Sadly, my respite was short-lived, since upon hearing the name "Maisie," being called from the neighboring house, she left me. The voice was moving toward the house's front door, and although I was tempted to stay and introduce myself, I remembered my condition and worried that detection would ruin any chance I had at developing an acquaintance with the neighbor, and by extension, any hope of learning more about this most splendid Maisie. I tried to unlock my door, but the adrenaline was such that I couldn't get the key in the lock before I was forced to abandon the task due to the opening of the neighbor's door, and instead, I dove for cover beside the hedges that separated our property. It was only when I heard the door closing behind them that my adrenaline faded enough for me to make a most consequential discovery.

The Introduction

What I discovered was an erection.

If that's a problem for you, as it was for me, and you find yourself unwilling to continue further, I ask that you first read the treatise "On Zoophilia" in the appendix, where many of your potential concerns will be addressed. As further reassurance, I'll quote a line from it, my law of zoophilia: "Any animal that is large enough to not suffer from a sexual act is too large to safely perform one with."

I waddled to my door, my pelvis thrust back in an attempt to mitigate the pain from the constraint imposed by my jeans upon my penis, as well as to prevent the discovery of the erection by any potential onlookers; that they wouldn't have possibly known the cause didn't occur to me, I was so wracked with horror and shame. Once inside, I slid down and unzipped my pants, not to masturbate, but to relieve the pressure.

As I sat there, staring at the erection and pondering its significance, I began to excuse it away, as if my ego was trying to avoid having to incorporate into itself a latent zoophilia. I remembered that the penis could, in the absence of sexual arousal, be brought to erection by physical stimulation alone; thus, I told myself that I'd probably experienced some chafing during the run and was too distracted to notice its effects. I readily accepted this explanation, and as my hyperventilating began to subside, I saw the erection drooping. Had I left it there, I could have gone the rest of my life without being forced to grapple with my hidden desires, but self-assured, I allowed myself to think of Maisie again if only to further prove she had nothing to do with it. Oddly enough, our meeting was as vivid in hindsight, and once my feelings returned, I noticed they brought with them another stiffy.

If I had a knife on me, I'd have cut it off, so disgusted was I by its presence, and what it implied of me. Horny for a dog? Am I losing my mind? I decided to masturbate to get rid of the erection, all the while policing my thoughts for any that might lead, even tangentially, to contemplations of things canine. Temporarily restored to sanity by ejaculation, I resumed thinking of Maisie, to discover the cause of my attraction. I'd seen dogs all my life but had never reacted like this. I thought there must be something special about this dog and that I could prevent further mishaps by avoiding her, sweet though she was. With time, my erection would take its place among the other unfortunate realities I'd come to ignore about myself.

I picked up Dante, hoping that rereading my favorite bits would put me in a better frame of mind—one less likely to bring about erotic ideations—but my mind wandered; each time I caught myself, I worried about where it would wander off to. I labored on, fighting back the thoughts of Maisie by staying occupied—showering, shaving, cleaning, cooking—but boredom would set in, and my mind would go off on tangents again. By early evening, I'd decided to return to the liquor store before it closed and get enough drinks to numb myself. I figured I'd get drunk enough to render thought impossible and effectively fast-forward through each day until I could trust my mind again.

Before leaving the house, worried I might run into Maisie and her owner, I scanned the neighborhood as best I could through the front windows and the peephole. Had it not been for this delay, I might have been in the clear; however, as is my luck, their doorway lights came on as I was passing. Frantic, I picked up my pace, walking as fast as I could without drawing attention, when I heard a "Hey!" coming from behind me.

I kept walking, hoping the shout was directed toward someone else, and though I soon learned that to be the case, that served as no relief; a second, more panicked yell impelled me to turn around. Maisie must have slipped away as her owner was locking the door and was halfway down the block before she'd noticed. For a second, I thought Maisie was running to me, rendering me too stunned to hear the owner's cries for help, but before reaching me, she veered toward the road. I dove to grab her faster than her owner could muster a shriek.

Taking hold of her leash, either because of her playful boisterousness or my befuddlement, was impossible, and I was forced to hold on to her. Her owner was upon us within seconds, but she didn't arrive soon enough to prevent me from succumbing to the contemplation of the feeling brought by her fur rubbing against me; had I not been startled by her owner's arrival, I might have moaned.

My mind was awash with concerns over the potential appearance of a hard-on or a recognition, on the part of the owner, of my desires, so I couldn't hear much of what she was saying until, turning to Maisie, the owner said, "She likes you." These words seemed to cut through my befuddlement, and I turned to Maisie and knelt to pet her and submit myself to her licking. This wasn't a conscious attempt at sneaking in some physical gratification, but rather an unintellectualized (possibly unintellectualizible) response to the joy I seemed to bring her merely by my presence. It was probably the first time in my life that I truly felt as if I could do no wrong, but it was short-lived, as that all-too-familiar pressure on the front of my pants alerted me to the emergence of yet another boner.

Maisie's owner probably attributed my sudden stiffness (of body, not penis) to an annoyance toward the dog, and yanking on her leash, got her to back away from me. She yelped from the sudden garrotting, and my heart sank as I saw her tail tucked between her legs. Had the owner known how close I was to strangling her with the leash in turn, she likely wouldn't have engaged me in neighborly small talk for as long as she did. But it seems her desire to be acquainted with this handsome, heroic new neighbor of hers was such that, when I mentioned the imminent closing of the liquor store and my need to depart, she chose to accompany me, though the neighborhood's walking trail was in the opposite direction.

With each stride, my penis would be contorted, and the pain was so great that I had to lie about forgetting my wallet so that I could cut the trip short. The owner seemed to want to follow me home too, so to get rid of her, I suggested that we meet again soon and get to know each other better, a promise I intended to put off until, insulted, she would lose interest. She mentioned a business trip in a few days, and after rambling about the exorbitant amount she'd have to spend on a dog hotel, she proposed waiting until after the trip to meet. I readily accepted, despite thinking only of the mention of a doggy hotel.

Agreeing that it was a waste of money and offering my dog-sitting services for free, I thought, meant that I could ensure continued opportunities to bask in Maisie's presence under the guise of helping out a neighbor. I blurted out the offer thoughtlessly, and it excited her enough to pull me into a hug, which I had to end quickly for fear that she might discover my erection rubbing against her and think herself the cause. She gave me her number, insisting that I tag along on their walk the next day to learn the route, which, despite being somewhat annoying, as it meant it'd be harder to blow her off, at least gave me the opportunity, in asking how to spell her name—*R-A-N-A*, as it turned out—to make up for having been too self-conscious to hear it earlier.

I walked until she was out of view, then I stopped to sit on a bus bench, gleeful at the success of my manipulation and the prospect of a full week with Maisie. Though thinking of it in the abstract—the opportunity to be with the one who made me feel so alive—was exhilarating, when my mind finally turned to specifics, I grew distraught and horrified at what I was planning. The emotional elevation I'd experienced from my encounter with Maisie served to increase the intensity of my self-chastisement, making it all the more gut-wrenching; thus, I could only think to go to the liquor store as fast as possible, hoping that the deadening effect of the alcohol would dampen the self-attacks. I charted a route on my phone that I was sure would steer me clear of Rana and Maisie and bought as many bottles as I could carry. I was even too distraught to torment the cashier as I had planned.

Though I didn't question my intentions as I drank, I wonder, in retrospect, if I hadn't been drinking to keep the attacks going, as opposed to numbing myself to them until their passing, since sobriety, as evidenced by the anguish I had felt when these thoughts returned on that bus bench, rendered thinking about my shortcomings—perceived or actual—incredibly painful, such that it almost forced me to rectify them or search for a different, more circumspect way of construing things. On the other hand, in a drunken stupor, my thoughts could be allowed to run wild indefinitely without the need for any real attempts to improve and/or reframe things. In general, my feelings of guilt and shame were things I wanted to avoid, and in thinking about the actions that elicited them and the flawed trains of thought that caused me to suffer unnecessarily because of them, I hoped to build a life in which those pangs came less often. But because my ego had realigned itself such that I saw myself as a horrible person, the innate desire to flee from pain was in conflict with my desire to experience it, since that sort of existential punishment seemed fitting. There would be moments when I'd wonder if I was self-destructive, but those were fleeting since they weren't in line with my new self-conception as a perverted wretch; my behavior, I thought, is what could reasonably be expect from a person as fucked up as me. Whatever the ultimate cause of my binge drinking, it resulted in my feeling, upon entering my bed, an onset of nausea, more intense than the bursts of queasiness I felt after each downed mouthful of whiskey (the drink I thought most suitable), and although I was hesitant to give in to it for fear that I might sober up, I vomited and cried myself to sleep.

I awoke to a text from Rana, inviting me to join them for a walk in a half hour, and after spending a few minutes trying to find the most palatable wording, I sent her a text rescinding my offer. She called me in seconds, outraged, saying she'd already cancelled her booking at the pet hotel. Her anger built as she explained to me the difficulty she had in arranging it and the impossibility, because of the hotel's popularity with friendless yuppie dog owners, of re-booking, until, worried she might come over and murder me, I agreed to go through with it. I tried to assure myself that having gone twenty-five years without any dog lust, I could go a week more without any, but the nagging sensation that what was sparked by our meeting could be set aflame by a week together led me to think that I'd have to sell the house and move to prevent any chance of my being pulled into an intractable love. I pushed back from that, thinking it extreme, and considered instead some new ways of controlling my impulses.

During my period of disillusionment, in an attempt to stave off what I thought was going to be a nervous breakdown, I did some research into meditation. I assumed those attempts failed because the task of clearing the mind isn't possible for one cursed with a mind as effervescent as mine, but I wondered if I should try again, as it might be a useful tool in suppressing any urges that might arise during my week with Maisie. I soon realized, however, that the state I was aiming for was the state that Maisie's presence had forced me into, and sliding back into my egoic negativity, I thought instead that what I needed was a mind so full of self-denouncements that any zoophilic ideations would be drowned out before they could manifest in another woody.

I allowed myself to think about my feelings toward her while closely monitoring myself for any arousal, the detection of which would be followed by a bout of self-flagellation with a cat-o'-nine-tails I had made by taking apart an Ethernet cord. Although I hoped that the pain would allow me to associate my lascivious thoughts about the dog with physical pain, all I managed to accomplish was adding to my depravity an element of sadomasochism; I knew I was on the wrong track when I caught myself daydreaming that I was a patch of dirt on which she'd urinate.

It occurred to me that introspection and an increased understanding of this facet of my character might help elucidate a solution, so I tried rewinding my life in search for any earlier signs of my zoophilia that had gone unnoticed. Unfortunately, my navel-gazing didn't present me with any epiphanic moments, and my desire for one drove me up a wall. I remembered having begged my father for a dog, and although I always thought it was motivated by jealousy of the other kids who had dogs of their own, I wondered not only whether my tantrum had been an early manifestation of my zoophilia, but also whether my zoophilia was genetic, and thus my father's aversion to getting me a dog had stemmed from his own indecorous urges.

These thoughts distracted me from our text conversation, and frustrated by my lack of replies, Rana called, insisting I join her and Maisie on the walk. Unable to muster up an excuse, I agreed, thinking I could survive one outing. It helped to tell myself that any lapses into lechery during this introductory walk would, at the very least, give me information with which I could improve my defenses in the days until the trip. I hoped that engaging Rana in conversation would keep my mind off Maisie, but since the entire point of the excursion was for me to learn more about her—preferences and routines, etc.—that proved impossible. Thankfully, I had worn looser trousers, and my tumescence was at least clandestine and painless.

I did learn a bit about Maisie's history. She'd been purchased by Rana's ex-boyfriend, Chip, who, I was told, was an eminent douche. The impetus for his purchase of the dog wasn't a fondness for dogs or the husky breed in particular, but rather the thought that wolves look cool, and that a husky would be the closest he could come to owning one. But ownership of Maisie got old, like his relationship with Rana, and he abandoned them both. Since then, Rana had been living in the house she'd purchased with marriage in mind, trying to build a life for herself while taking care of a dog whose tendency to remind her of what was and could have been, I imagined, had sown within her the seeds of contempt.

The walk was proceeding well when, during my stint at holding the leash, things took a sharp turn. We came into contact with another dog, a friend of Maisie's, I learned, who, walking up to her and sniffing her rear, proceeded to mount her as the two dog owners conversed. I pushed the beast off in a fit of jealous rage and yanked Maisie's leash, both to get her away from her suitor as well as to punish her for tormenting me. It created a bit of an uproar, but I attributed my outburst to a fear that Maisie might not have been spayed, and the matter was laughed off. I felt my fury building back up as I stared, transfixed, at the frolicking of the two dogs, so I diverted my attention by engaging Rana and the owner of that lecherous dog in small talk.

I failed to take into account the seeming inability of dog owners, at least when in each other's company, to carry on conversations about anything other than their dogs, and I was forced to learn more about this transgressor than I'd otherwise liked to have known. I was told, jovially, that my rival—Quincey was his name—who was again sniffing my Maisie's rear in the interregnum between bouts of humping, hadn't had a decline in his libido since his recent neutering. I wondered if giving him the penectomy he deserved would put an end to his humping once and for all, but I managed to prevent myself from administering it, though I wasn't able to fake a laugh as well as Rana.

My anger began to die down as I realized that it made no sense for me to begrudge Quincey something that I desired myself; that he could act so freely on it, and that I was restrained by a societal stigma more restrictive than any leash, was no fault of his. What made this scene so jarring was the ease with which Maisie had given herself up to this canine lothario. But if I were to be angry, surely it should be directed toward the one who, through her casual handing out of the affection I'd come to cherish, denigrated both herself, for exposing her coquettish nature, and more importantly, me, for having been foolish enough to place such value on something so worthless as to be offered to any passerby. Thankfully, my fledgling love for Maisie made me unable to dwell too long on any failing of hers, and my jealousy wasn't able to fester.

My mind turned to those graces of hers that made both Quincey and me her servants, and my feelings toward Quincey transformed from animosity to vicarious joy. Thrilled though I came to be at witnessing my cuckolding, it did not leave my mind that, unlike Quincey, my enjoyment could never be had so freely, and my joy was always tempered with a hint of horror at betraying myself by smiling. I wondered if any emotion so pleasant as to manifest in an innocent smile should be repressed, especially by one for whom a smile proved to be such a profound relief; nevertheless, I allowed myself to watch the dogs have sex again.

It occurred to me that the only tranquillity I'd felt since my epiphany came during either the undistracted moments in Maisie's presence or the time spent thinking about her. What both states had in common was that time spent within them seemed to add to their momentum, as if being near her or thinking of her necessarily meant a further entanglement. What, then, could that feeling of bliss that accompanies both be but an innate enticement?

That I had an erection there could be no doubt, but what I planned to do with it, on the other hand, proved difficult to ascertain. Despite the arousal I got from watching Quincey in action, I knew that it wouldn't do to merely supplant him, since my ignorance of the dimensions of the canine vagina meant I couldn't be certain it wouldn't cause her harm, but I wasn't sure if my desires were entirely voyeuristic or more carnal in nature. Having heard that the application of peanut butter to one's genitals could induce a dog to lick, replicating human-human oral sex, I started to daydream about it—so vividly, in fact, that had it not been for the tape with which I had secured my penis to my thigh, my erection, throbbing to the point of explosion, would have almost certainly been noticed. Disgusted at myself for working out the logistics of so heinous an act, however, I forced myself to stop this train of thought. What difference would it make if the peanut butter was smooth or crunchy if the cost of applying it was one's humanity?

Since these machinations began with the impulse to succumb to my desires, I resumed the task of fighting them off. I told myself that these emotions were not a respite, but the siren's song of my inner zoophile, and that true relief would come with the satisfaction of knowing, upon Rana's return from her business trip, that I had managed to keep from doing anything bestial. I hoped also that by congratulating myself for fighting off any urges, I'd mitigate the stress of the constant self-shaming, making my condition bearable.

Too weak-willed to maintain vigilance, I failed, for the remainder of that walk and ultimately, during the days that followed, to exile the fantasy of the peanut butter blow job from my mind completely. It seemed the perfect way to experiment during my upcoming stay with Maisie: victimless, low risk of detection, easily doable. Driving it out of my mind didn't undo the thoughts I'd already had, and I'd pick up my planning, adding more and more detail to my fantasies, making them all the more appealing; in time, my desire to explore my feelings became as strong as my disgust toward them.

Dog Sitting

My eagerness to explore my sexuality was nowhere to be found when I woke up on the day of Rana's departure; I looked at the jars of peanut butter I'd fished out of the garbage twice the previous night with pointed disgust. I could throw them away, I thought, but I couldn't throw away temptation itself; no matter what I did, within fifteen minutes, an era of my life would begin, before the close of which I might lose myself entirely.

Although I thought my passing the test a possibility, the knowledge that I'd been preparing for a tryst, not a trial, undermined any confidence I had in my self-control, and failure, I felt, would relegate me to a life of shame, in comparison to which death seemed inviting. Complementary to this suicidal impulse was a disinterestedness with regard to my death, a product of my generalized self-loathing; as I came to see myself as abhorrent, my suicide began to seem like a favor to society. Pushed to action by Rana's imminent arrival, I scurried to my car, hoping to run it in the garage and suffocate myself with its emissions.

As soon as I turned the car on, however, I heard Maisie's barking close by, and Rana opened my garage door and walked over to me. "Not trying to skip out on me, are you?" she said with a laugh as she pulled Maisie over to the driver's side window.

Without allowing me time to take hold of the leash, she raced out, saying her cabbie was out front. I jumped out of the car for fear that Maisie would follow her into the road, but she didn't leave my side. I hoped to tie her to my porch, where she'd be safe from the car's fumes, and return to kill myself, but Maisie wouldn't budge. It struck me as off that a dog who'd heretofore been so pliant would put up such resistance, and when I tried to force her, I got a sharp snarl. For a second, I thought she knew what I was planning to do in the garage, but I brushed that off and set to killing myself before any other fanciful notions weakened my resolve.

Going through with the car method would mean killing Maisie too, so I looked for an alternative—the electric drill I'd been using for home improvement. I went inside to get it, but Maisie was already in the doorway when I tried to shut the door behind me, and I was forced to let her in. I knew that I couldn't kill myself and leave her trapped inside until Rana's return, but I was still set on suicide. Leaving the door ajar seemed possible, but I knew it'd open me up to the possibility that some Good Samaritan, hearing my screams, might seek medical aid—I'm sure the damage inflicted by the drill would have limited the doctor's ability to save me, but I couldn't risk them bringing me to a condition stable enough that people would be able to inquire as to my reasoning. In the end, I decided to install a makeshift doggy door and leave out a bag of dog food before going through with the trepanning.

Construction of the doggy door should have been easy enough, but the task was made almost impossible by the persistent harassment I'd suffered at Maisie's paw. No sooner would I place a tool down, than she would carry it off. Assuming her restlessness stemmed from not having a morning walk, I took her for a stroll to quiet her down.

Unfortunately, we ran into Quincey and his owner, and despite my efforts to feign unrecognition and pull Maisie along, the two dogs pulled us toward each other. I tried to keep the interaction brief, but Quincey's owner proved unable to take a hint, and I was forced to stay with him, listening to his rambling while trying desperately to keep from inadvertently divulging my agitation. His talking didn't even help me keep my attention away from the dogs, since his droning on about the history books he'd been reading and the college football scores was so dull that my mind seemed to flee to the consideration of them.

It probably would have been wiser for me to have looked at them because their activities could not have been more provocative than the images my mind generated of hot dog-on-dog action. I'd managed to defy the urge to peek, but the dog's tussling led to the intertwining of the leashes, forcing me to look right at them.

As Quincey's owner and I danced an awkward two-step to try and keep a knot from forming, I felt that tell-tale pressure against the front of my pants yet again. Although most of my attention went to ensuring that my erection didn't graze Quincey's owner, lest he interpret it as my response to his analysis of the sixteenth-century cotton market and I find myself in a fight with more than just my libido, I had enough of my mind free to realise that the pain throbbing throughout my groin was a fitting punishment for such aberrant arousal.

Once we freed our leashes of the entanglement, I returned home, my will to die fully reinvigorated. I resumed construction, but contrary to my expectations, the walk did nothing to reduce Maisie's forestalling. Furious, I tethered her to the railing of a stairwell a safe distance away, and though my heart broke at the sound of her whimpers, I turned a deaf ear to them and only let her go once the doggy door was finished.

As soon as she was free, she pounced upon me, tail wagging and licking me as if I hadn't just been her jailor. Although I felt my heart well up, I stoically took up the drill and plugged it in. After inserting the sharpest drill bit, I closed my eyes and placed the tip of the bit against my temple. It took me a few seconds to work up the courage to pull the trigger, but once I did, nothing happened. Annoyed, I opened my eyes to find that Maisie had pulled the cord out. I tried to snatch it, but she gnawed through it before I could.

Almost angry enough to kick her but unable to bring myself to do it, I instead fashioned a noose from what was left of the cord, intending to attach it to a ceiling beam. But as I tried to mount the stool I was using as a makeshift stepladder, Maisie pushed it over. I made more progress on my second attempt by swatting her away with one hand while I climbed and secured the noose, but before I placed my neck inside, she lunged at me and knocked me clear over.

I awoke to Maisie's licking me, and for just a moment, after the return of consciousness but before the return of conscience, I allowed her tongue to brush over me. I felt that soothing sensation that came over me when we met, but my bliss repulsed me, and I pushed her off; unable to cope with the dysphoria, I lay there and wept. Even this, however, Maisie wouldn't leave uninterrupted, and she continued her constant licking.

I pulled back to avoid it, enraged that she could be playful at a time like this; I glowered at her, but catching the sight of her eyes, I couldn't see a hint of playfulness. What I saw instead was a steady gaze, under which I felt thoroughly exposed; there was also a softness, and even a warmth in her eyes that made me feel as if, not only could she see me to the core, but she liked me nonetheless. Why, I didn't for the life of me know, but it made me wonder if I wasn't all that bad.

I also saw—not in her eyes, but in her actions throughout the day—a recognition of my plight and an effort to save me from myself. I laughed it off as crazy, but then Maisie started licking me again, and my open mouth allowed her tongue in. After a slight tilt of my head, my tongue was inside hers, too. I pulled her into my lap, holding her tight with one hand, while the other caressed first her face, then worked its way down to her hind leg.

Most other acts possible between us would have found Maisie at a disadvantage, but the sheer size of her tongue, which filled my mouth almost entirely, put us on an even level. Eager to explore every crevice of her mouth, I was too excited to remember to breathe and only pulled back when the palpitations of my heart began to tinge my ecstasy with fear that, unable to contain my swelling feelings, I'd have a heart attack. Even then, I only paused long enough to regain enough stillness and breathe in enough air that I could go in for another kiss.

During those breaks I'd remember the times I failed to kiss her when kissing her was the only thing I wanted to do, and I set to making up for those mistakes: I thought about the moment we met and the emotional one-eighty I made and kissed her in thanks. I dwelt upon Rana's taking the leash before our first walk together, which made Maisie, recognizing the coming of a walk, wag her tail and pant gleefully, and I tried to channel that vicarious excitement for her into another kiss. I even thought about tugging at her leash, jealous of Quincey, and kissed her in awe of her capacity for forgiveness.

Once I'd exhausted the memories formed in our short time together, I shifted to daydreaming about our future. I imagined her where she was, looking at me with the same unbridled affection, even though her face was being caressed by liver-spotted hands. As the heat of passion died down and the strain of the day took its toll, I imagined a tiny puppy lying asleep between us, for whom my heart overflowed with fondness while we drifted off to sleep.

I woke up first, which allowed me to bask in her beauty; she looked so angelic that I was tempted to wake her up to continue kissing her. I detected, however, the presence of morning wood, which put an end to my reveries; I thought that kisses of the kind Maisie and I had shared the night before occur on a more philosophical and emotional plane than their physicality implies, and an erection seemed to sully it all. I hoped a cold shower would get rid of it and afford me some time to think.

Standing there, with the shower head pointed toward my crotch and forcing myself not to back away from the cold water, I watched with relief as my penis shriveled back down; however, I knew I wasn't out of the woods just yet. An erection is not like an alarm clock with a snooze button that can be hit, pushing things back to a more convenient time. An erection necessitates action; I would have to ejaculate eventually.

I planned to watch human-human pornography when I next noticed an erection, which was immediately upon returning to Maisie and finding her awake. I took out my phone and then my penis, and proceeded to sift through thumbnails, but although the porn site's algorithms had heretofore been adept at predicting what I'd like, the recommendations, not taking into account the changes in my "taste profile," weren't doing it for me. I only felt arousal during my cursory glances at Maisie, and with the previous day's self-loathing returning, I ran into another room.

I tried meditative masturbation, focusing only on the feeling of my hand against my penis, but it didn't bring about climax; thus, I found myself with a penis both stiff and sore, and a mind that percolated with thoughts of Maisie. I decided to take another cold shower and then purchase some ice packs from the local pharmacy to ward off further erections until I could find a solution.

It seemed prudent to use the trek as an opportunity to take Maisie on a walk, but that proved to be unwise since her excitement when taken outside brought back my erection. I compounded the problem by making an unplanned stop at a coffee shop to pick up breakfast, where Maisie, always the center of attention, was showered by patrons with pats and snuggles that—had I given them—could only have been the prelude to another bout of passionate making out. Hurrying to the restroom, I inserted an ice pack into my pants and returned home, intent on keeping the ice pack in place until I either had a plan or detected the onset of nerve damage.

Once home, I took out some loose-leaf paper, thinking that I might exorcise my emotions and convince myself of their insanity by writing, but my mind took instead to philosophizing on the dichotomy between love and sex. Those thoughts are summarized in my essay, "On Zoophilia," which is a distillation of the writing I did that day, so I won't repeat them here, but suffice it to say that after realizing the erection was borne of intimacy, not lust, I was so full of love toward my penis, the manifestation of my affection, that I wanted to bend over and kiss it.

Lacking the required flexibility, I instead threw the ice pack off and waited, pants removed, for my erection's triumphant return. Until then, I intended to run the experiments I had devised the day before. They related to the peanut butter blow job, which, due to the frequency with which it will be referenced in the following paragraphs, I will shorten to *PBBJ*.

A PBBJ requires three things: a dog, some peanut butter, and an inordinate amount of faith—more faith than I had in Maisie, as it turned out, since my fantasies were always ruined by images of me lying dead in a pool of blood as she buried my bone in the yard. To mitigate these fears, I planned to present her with a peanut butter coated dildo, and later, depending on her reaction, my penis, similarly festooned.

She approached the dildo with trepidation, sniffing it for some time, but at last, she licked it. I nearly cried with joy at the sight and immediately slathered the peanut butter on my penis, but then she started to bite. I watched with horror as she held the dildo down with her front paws and proceeded to gnaw off the head. I was petrified. But then, done with the dildo, she turned to my penis, and I leaped back, running to the bathroom where I scrubbed the peanut butter off. Needless to say, I was no longer erect.

I suppose it could be said that my experiment was flawed, and Maisie would have reacted differently to an actual penis, especially one attached to her lover, but I had no desire to inquire further; instead, I tried to devise an alternate way to induce ejaculation. I thought of getting a paw job, but her digital pads were so rough, I feared I'd become the first man to be circumcised via chafing. It soon became clear that my affair with Maisie would be one defined by the contemplation of her perfection, punctuated by violent bouts of masturbation.

I was too traumatized by the mauling of the dildo to take my penis out in Maisie's presence and would scurry to another room to masturbate whenever aroused, but the vividness of my memory and my capacity for fantasizing quickly proved wanting, and I required visual aids. Her presence being the perfect fix, I accustomed myself to being erect around her, masturbating under a blanket while staring at her, then removing it with her safely on the other side of a room, gradually growing in confidence with each step until I felt safe masturbating while making out with her. This could have been enough, had I not discovered during one of our walks that even more bliss was possible.

Although she was always intoxicating for me to be near, her demeanor in the house, which was usually sluggish, wasn't as exciting as watching her in the park, especially seeing the coquetry she displayed whenever she'd see Quincey. If, however, I managed to surreptitiously record her rendezvous with Quincey, I could watch the clips with her as we cuddled and made out; I was sure that this would have been exciting for her, since in addition to pleasing me, she'd be able to relive the moments with Quincey. Balancing between the quality of the films and the discretion with which they could be made, I decided to purchase a watch with a built-in camera, thinking that by tilting my hand along with the movement of the leash, I could track Maisie effectively. It took some practice for me to be able to keep the action in frame while not looking at her, but I was soon ready to take her out for another walk.

God bless this man, Quincey's owner, for his verbosity and tangential—almost to the point of schizophrenic—manner of storytelling, which so extended our conversation that I was able to record nearly a half hour on our first walk. He so delighted in being listened to, for what was apparently the first time in his life, that getting him to keep talking was no trouble; I'd ask for a clarification and he'd give me a dissertation, or if he commended a historian, I'd ask which other books he'd recommend by her. Sadly, within time, Maisie and Quincey, apparently growing tired of each other, ceased fucking.

Eager to go home and spank it to the footage, I realized I had gotten Quincey's owner going too far and had to take great pains to extricate myself from the discussion. Merely remaining silent and looking bored wasn't enough, as he had long since stopped listening to or even looking at me; I was pretty sure I could have walked away unnoticed for at least a few minutes, but fearing that such an insult might prevent any further opportunities for recording, I decided against it. Instead, I lied about forgetting to turn off the oven, which despite not being enough to get him to shut up, at least got us headed in the direction of my house.

There was one benefit, however, in his insisting on following me: his company was better than any ice pack in suppressing an erection, and the walk home was my least painful walk since being smitten. It would have been perfect if he hadn't, under the assumption that we had become friends, asked me out for drinks. I found the idea thoroughly revolting, but I knew I couldn't say no without him ducking me in the dog park, so I agreed, comforting myself with the knowledge that bloviating and awkward though he was, he could easily be induced into serving as a window into the lives and histories of Maisie and

Rana, revealing information that might have seemed inappropriate to one who, unlike him, wasn't unfamiliar with all social norms.

Once home, after dimming the lights and turning on some mood music, I played the recordings, but sexually stimulating though they were, their quality—the shakiness, blurriness, wind noise—left me yearning to see it first-hand; thus, it was clear that I needed to find out how to masturbate unnoticed in the dog park. Cutting a hole in the pocket of a trench coat would be the easy part; what I'd need to work on was being able to jerk off without the motion of my arm becoming apparent, as well as keeping a straight face while climaxing. I spent all night masturbating in the mirror and was soon able to ejaculate without betraying anything more than slight detachment, staring off at nothing like a folk singer.

The next meet-up with Quincey and his owner lasted a full hour, in which time I masturbated so much that my ejaculate had begun to seep through my clothing. Furious at myself for not devising a semen sequestration mechanism, I broke off our conversation and hurried home, trying to obscure the wet spot. Quincey's owner reiterated his invitation, proposing that evening as a prime opportunity, but even if he weren't a total bore, I'd have said no, for that night was my last with Maisie.

I couldn't imagine returning to a lonely life any more than I could understand how I had managed to live so long without her; shameful as it is to admit, I caught myself wishing for a plane accident to extend Maisie's stay permanently, but my self-castigation at thinking such a terrible mishap should befall Rana was mitigated by the remembrance of how sweet that week was. I knew I'd miss the mornings the most, for they did more than anything to improve my outlook; a day that started with Maisie in my arms was assuredly one in which, even if my self-loathing reared its head, I'd have enough of a reservoir of happiness that not even I could deplete. If that day ended, as all those days had, with us similarly entwined, then I could get through the night without my negativity bleeding into my dreams.

I had found, it appeared, my indefatigable happiness, but it was only possible when she was mine, which she would never be again. On the final morning, I tried to keep our cuddling going as long as possible; when my phone vibrated, though I knew it was Rana informing me of her arrival, I ignored it in favor of caressing Maisie's fur. I even ignored the honking of a car in my driveway and a loud knock on my door, but when a man's voice called my name, I couldn't keep Maisie from leaping up, wagging her tail as she ran toward the door. I had trouble unlocking the door, as Maisie was clawing at it boisterously, but once I did and she scurried out, bringing a burst of laughter from the man outside, I knew our honeymoon was over.

Rana and Chip

I waited before stepping out myself, so as to miss any displays of affection between the two, but I mistimed it; I was forced to watch Maisie licking this villain as he laughed, blissfully unaware of my death stare. Seeing Quincey with my beloved was one thing, since I could convince myself it was just physical, but seeing her with another man was too much. Although he did not seem to be kissing her with the same passion as me, it irked me nonetheless. I forced my eyes away and saw Rana carrying luggage inside. I offered my assistance and after inquiring about her trip, asked about the man on my porch. "That's Chip, my boyfriend."

"Ex-boyfriend?" I asked, hoping to have caught her in a slip. She smiled, and looking over at him and Maisie lovingly, explained that they were trying to work things out. I could sense that she was trying to suppress her hope, and wanting to seem like a good friend, I did my best to feign excitement, but that proved hard to do; I knew that Chip's re-entry into Rana's life would render my dog-sitting services unnecessary. I struggled to find a way to sabotage their reunion, but to do so effectively, I'd need to know more about their relationship, especially their break up. I briefly introduced myself to Chip before rushing back inside to go over my options.

Rana had mentioned, after our first walk, that she'd befriended Quincey's owner shortly after her break-up with Chip and that he'd been a source of comfort to her, so my first order of business became taking him up on that offer for drinks. I hoped he might have some insights that, if I was able to steer the conversation away from the usual inane lectures, I'd be able to use to my advantage. So, I called up Quincey's owner and, eager as always to have someone to talk to other than his dog, he agreed to see me for drinks that night.

I arrived early so that he could find me at the bar, sullen and already drinking. I told him I was upset about Rana and Chip dating again, but in actuality, I was thinking about Maisie's possible forced estrangement in hopes that, my emotion being real, he wouldn't believe the explanation fake. To keep him from thinking my agitation was a friend's concern, I told him that it was borne out of an intense love I'd been harboring for Rana. I beseeched him to be my Friar Laurence.

Assuring him I was only asking so that, temporarily unable to be her lover, I could at least be a competent friend to Rana, I poked around her history. He shed some light on Rana's reaction to the split; she'd considered herself lucky to no longer have to put up with Chip's jealousy, which seemed like my way in. He must have promised her that he'd work on it, but I was sure I could convince her that he'd be incapable of growth. "Oh, Rana," I could hear myself saying, "can't you see that some men aren't emotionally equipped to deal with the pressures of dating a woman as beautiful as you?"

But I felt it was too early to plan the conversation. Not only did I have to survive this outing with Quincey's owner, where dying of boredom was a real possibility, but I'd also have to ingrain myself into Rana and Chip's lives enough that my advice wouldn't come unsolicited. As a first step, I bought some wine on the way home, hoping to ply them with drinks and win their friendship. I'd parked my car and was about to walk over to Rana's door when Chip emerged from within. He wasn't staying over, it appeared, and disappointed as I was that my manipulation would have to be delayed, I took succor in the fact that it at least meant I would have more time to work with than I had thought initially.

I kept my eyes fixed on the door, hoping that I'd be able to get my first glimpse of Maisie in almost half a day; the longing I felt was just a preview, I thought, of a life cut off from her, but I was sure I'd never allow that to be the case. My yearning was such that when Maisie came out to lick Chip goodbye, none of my anger and jealousy landed on her; instead, it was all channeled into an increased hatred of Chip.

If Chip did win Rana back, there was a possibility that she—and more importantly, Maisie—would be living with him, so I thought it might serve me well to know where he lived, ensuring I'd able to see her in that contingency; I laid back to avoid detection as he got into his car and pulled out, then I followed him at a distance. It seemed a bit strange to me that I was stalking a man I'd just met, but the importance of my mission overpowered those inklings, and I followed him all the way to his home.

I planned to return to my home after writing down his address, but it occurred to me that this was a great chance to get information about Chip that I could use in winning his friendship. I checked the Internet for the location of the nearest sporting goods shop and drove over to procure some binoculars. Upon returning to his house, however, I found him entering his car, dressed for a night out. I followed again, this time to a bar, and hoping to snap some photos of him with another woman that I could present to Rana as being taken during their attempted reunion, I waited near the window his booth was beside.

It was, as I expected, a woman who joined him, but although she seemed to expect an embrace, there was none forthcoming that I could capture with my camera. I don't know who was more disappointed, her or me, and I grew desperate to overhear their conversation. I went inside, careful not to make my face visible to Chip—even though he was too focused on keeping his interlocutor from crying to notice anyone else—and sat as close to them as I thought safe. From what I gathered, they had met during Rana and Chip's hiatus, and until that moment, neither woman knew of the other's existence.

The poor woman could only remark on Chip's sudden change in demeanor; gone was the vibrant man she had met. Her ignorance of this colder side of him wasn't due to concealment on his part, but was a natural consequence of his feelings for her. She made him so happy that she'd never seen him feel anything else, but when he'd written that happiness off as yet another childish dalliance, he hardened his heart to her so as to do what he thought mature.

Saint that she was, she didn't mention her pain. Instead, she expressed admiration for what seemed to be a genuine desire on his part to get his relationship with Rana to work. Although I shared this approbation, it wasn't enough to stop me from wanting to smother that relationship in the cradle. They said their goodbyes, and after giving her sufficient time to cry alone, I approached to buy her a drink.

She was wary of me, assuming that I was trying to prey on her while she was weak, and she politely declined. I told her that I'd recognized in her the same heartbreak I'd been suffering from and offered her, in myself, a commiserator. She accepted my offer of a drink and my company, but not my assurances that talking about the man causing her anguish would be cathartic; I had to set the tone with some vulnerability of my own, so I made up a story of being recently rejected. I told her I'd tried to get back a woman I'd left to take another shot with my on-again/off-again girlfriend, but she'd been too dignified to accept me. She took my bait and was soon talking to me as if to a therapist.

They had met at an archery range, he an experienced hobbyist and she an interested beginner. Archery seemed like a perfect entryway into his life for me, too, so after asking her for the range's location, I purchased archery equipment on my phone while she was in the restroom. I'd pretend to have interest but not knowledge, putting Chip in the position of archery guru, which I knew he'd enjoy occupying. The hardest part would be not sending one of the arrows through him, but I didn't expect to be at the lessons long enough to develop the required skill.

I excused myself, citing a work meeting the following morning, and drove back to Chip's house to stake him out, but a yearning for Maisie rendered me a poor spy; though my eyes were glued to the binoculars, all I could see was her, and within time, Chip had fallen asleep without me learning much more. Driving home was itself fraught with danger, since I found myself drifting through lanes and idling after light changes; I knew I'd been away from Maisie too long, but alas, one cannot knock on one's neighbor's door in the wee hours of the morning and express a desire to spend time with their dog.

The best I could hope for was a repeat of my first interaction with Maisie: being opposite a door from her. It might seem like a small consolation, mere propinquity to one's lover, but at that moment, I could only wonder how such a bounty was wasted on me days before. I waited until all the lights went out in the area, and dressed in black, I snuck over to Rana's house.

Sitting down by Rana's back door, trying to avoid the porch light, I gave the door a little rap, then placed my ear on it. Within seconds I heard footfalls, which I deduced by their rapidity to be canine, and though I wanted to scream her name, I managed keep to whispering; I'd barely had time to take out my penis when she barked.

I heard more footfalls, heavier this time, and the kitchen lights came on. Afraid to take the time to put away my penis lest I be caught, I ran for home, erect with pants at mid-thigh. I'd made it to the hedge that separated our properties by the time Rana's door opened and managed to hop over without being detected by Rana or circumcised by the shrubs. Maisie ran out, and facing my direction, barked; I was confident that Rana wouldn't be able to see me, but continued noise, I worried, might wake the neighbors, who could easily spot me. Thankfully, Rana shushed her and dragged her back in. I put my flaccid penis away and went inside.

My penis, however, was not flaccid for long, as I began reviewing my dog park sex tapes. Though satisfying, the allure was already fading, and I knew I'd grow tired of them soon enough if they were my only sustenance night in and night out. I needed a way to see Maisie. I scanned her house with my binoculars, trying to find out where Maisie slept; I succeeded but could only see the tip of her tail through a crack in the curtain. If I could get in and move the dog bed just a foot to the side, I thought, I'd want for nothing.

From what I could see from my vantage point— the sofa and a piano—I assumed Maisie to be in Rana's living room. Entry into it should be easy enough to obtain, I figured, once I was on good enough terms with Rana to be invited inside; to set that ball rolling, all I had to do was apprise Rana of my newfound love of archery. The next morning, I sent her a text, explaining that I was expecting an item to be delivered that afternoon, and since I wasn't sure if I'd be around, I asked if she wouldn't mind it being left with her instead. I assured her that it wasn't heavy, just a composite bow, and she took the bait.

After a few texts, in which I expressed my interest in archery as well as my cluelessness about it, she insisted on setting me up with Chip for lessons. I told her I didn't want to impose, but she brushed it off, texting me his number, and informing me that she'd given him mine. With that, I got in my car and drove around aimlessly, hoping to kill time until I was notified of the bow's delivery.

During the ride I wondered if I might be wasting my life—I had no idea how much time had passed since I'd met her, or if I spent time thinking of anything else—and for the first time since Maisie saved me from suicide, my shame reemerged. This time, it wasn't so much about the desire for the dog, as I'd already embraced that, but the lengths I was going to—lying, manipulating, and even stalking— made me wonder if I wasn't a bit obsessive. That the love of one's life should be the most significant part of it made sense, but for it to be the only part seemed a bit insane. I wondered where this monomaniacal focus on her would lead and felt impelled to seek out more to occupy myself, but the text from Rana came before I found out what that would be, so I put it off and drove back.

She opened the door almost as soon as I rang the bell since she was just about to take Maisie out for a walk; I gently grabbed the leash, then told her she looked too tired to go out and offered to take Maisie instead. I could see her relief and followed up by offering to hold her for the rest of the day, but Rana was hesitant, saying that she couldn't ask more of me than I'd already done for her. Laughing, I told her I wouldn't mind, and she agreed; she was lucky she let go of the leash when she did because I'm not sure I'd have been able to force myself to let go of it had she resisted further.

She went inside, and after a quick stop at my house to drop off the bow and pick up my spy watch,

I took Maisie for a walk. It was the worst walk yet; Quincey was nowhere to be found, and of the male dogs we encountered, none were large enough to mount her, so making doggy porn was out of the picture. Hoping that if I couldn't see her engaging in licentious behaviour, I could at least see her happy, I led her to the leash-free area and watched her frolicking with other dogs. Thankfully, Chip called before I was locked into a conversation with the dog owners, and after he expressed his delight at learning about our shared passion, we arranged to have our first lesson the next day. Despite my attempts to end the conversation so I could focus instead on Maisie playing, Chip prated on about archery until the other dogs had tired out, and their owners dispersed.

Furious, I walked home, where I saw Rana in the yard with a woman I'd never seen; the woman soon walked to the curb, taking photographs of the house. Walking up to Rana, I pointed at the woman and knitted my brow in confusion, which she cleared up by saying, "She's the real estate agent; I'm putting the house up for sale."

"Oh, wow," was the best I could come up with, as my mind was in too much of a tumult for me to focus on making conversation; then the realtor walked over, and Rana broke away before I could add anything else. I staggered into my house with Maisie in tow, trying to hold it all in, but tears overwhelmed me as I was taking off my shoes, and I lay down by the doorway, bawling. Maisie tried to lick me but I pushed her away, shocked that she could think of making out at a time like this; the lack of concern regarding my consternation implicit in her randiness made me wonder if ours was a one-sided love, and when she came back, I shoved her with such force that she began to whimper. My anger gave way to worry, and I reached over to ensure that she wasn't hurt too badly; she recoiled slightly at my approach, and my shame brought on a fit of crying even worse than before, which thankfully elicited enough pity that she began licking anew.

I knew that though she loved me too, she didn't comprehend the value of her love, which is why she lavished it on that hound dog Quincey and that boorish Chip. This isn't because—as my more cynical readers might say—she's a dog, but a result of being raised by Rana, by whom Maisie's lovingness was neither recognized, nor reciprocated. It was therefore, I thought, up to me, who could see her loving nature and could appreciate the profundity of our union, to ensure that we would remain together. After some kissing, I let Maisie play with the mangled remains of the dildo so that I could figure out how to do that.

Murder, of course, was too extreme, and although its planning brought me a strange delight, I pushed it out of my mind as a waste of time. Dognapping came to mind—I'd tell Rana that Maisie ran away, keeping her hidden until any searches were abandoned and I was able to find new lodgings—but if someone began to suspect me, linking me to a disappearance would be too easy. An arrest was unthinkable. Although the writing of this book implies that I have no qualms about my name forever being associated with zoophilia, I wasn't as self-assured at the time, so I brushed the idea of dognapping off, too.

Although I didn't know if a move was imminent, I felt this development meant I wouldn't be able to forge as close a rapport with Chip as I had planned before twisting his mind; I reassured myself that with a bit of charm and the help of Chip's vapidity, he'd be primed for my manipulation soon enough. Though it seemed possible that Rana was selling in order to live with Chip, a circumstance that would allow me to catch glimpses of Maisie during stakeouts of his house, the knowledge that they'd only gotten back together recently gave me some doubt about Rana's intentions. Thankfully, I found an approach I hoped could confirm or rule out a move-in with Chip, get me more information, and damage their relationship all at the same time.

I waited to bring the move up during our lesson, passing the time with questions about proper form and a rant about both a fascination with medieval warfare and idolization of Robin Hood, which I said had attracted me to the sport. When the conversation drew to a lull, I changed gears: "So, Rana told me she's selling." He nodded, and giving it no thought, proceeded to line up a shot. I made myself out to be troubled, worried about the timing of the sell, and asked if he thought it wise.

He thought the timing inconsequential. "Sure, the market isn't great, but who's to say it won't get even worse? Plus, she's not exiting it completely; she's just switching homes."

Why is it that these rubes always jump to thoughts of money? "No, I meant between you two. I mean, I know it isn't my business, but isn't it a bit quick to be moving in together?" He laughed it off and aimed, but I patted him on the shoulder and pushed the bow down. "I'm not joking, man. I've been watching these true crime shows; every once in a while, you see a guy get axed by his girlfriend,"—more laughter—"and the guy doesn't notice the red flags because she got him to rush into things."

He laughed harder still. "Thanks for the concern, bud, but I think I'll be fine."

"Borderline personality disorder is a serious condition. You shouldn't be overconfident."

"Jesus Christ, what the fuck is wrong with you? Relax, all right? She's not moving in with me." Gone was the potential solace of at least seeing her through my binoculars; I'd have plunged into sorrow if I didn't need to pay attention to his words.

Rana had been planning this for some time, he told me. I realized she'd probably mentioned it on several occasions while I'd been busy ogling her dog, and I cursed my aloofness; had I known the banal occurrences of her life would have had such an impact on mine, I surely would have, but I supposed it was too late. I'd always believed that since language evolved as a means of transmitting information, talking to someone only made sense if done to extract it, but in the future, I'd remember to be more attentive, if only for my own sake.

"Has she found a new place?"

He looked at me askance, as if he thought I was prying but did tell me that she'd bought a condo near work and that "it's pretty nice."

I was too shaken up to take in anything else he said, let alone congratulate myself on a successful manipulation. A condo! To think, a dog as lively and majestic as Maisie confined to a condo! I could see her, my Maisie, confused—overwhelmed, even—by the onslaught of foreign noises and smells that she'd be subjected to, so disoriented that she'd bark uncontrollably at every passing of a neighbor by the door. Chip's lack of teaching skills saved Rana's life, for had I known how to shoot, I'd have gone to her house and killed her on the spot.

Chip's reaction to my last question meant I couldn't ask where work was, so I had to launch something of an investigation. People like her, thankfully, have everything about them available on the Internet, so the identity of her employer was only a few clicks away, but I'd first have to learn her last name. Therefore, in addition to moving Maisie's dog bed, I had to glance at Rana's mail the next time I was in her house.

I cut the lesson short, saying I'd promised Rana I'd have Maisie back soon. This was a lie, of course, since I'd been texting Rana an offer to hold Maisie for the night as she recovered from jetlag. My anxiety kept me from enjoying what I thought might be our last night together; I wasted valuable kissing time weeping on her withers. When she slept, I couldn't bring myself to cuddle her like before, so instead I figured out how I'd talk my way into Rana's house, as well as where to move the dog bed to provide the best view of Maisie. I studied the imperfections of the hardwood visible in the opening of the curtains with my binoculars and figured out exactly how far to nudge it and what angle to rotate it so that I'd see as much of her as possible.

The next morning, while dropping Maisie off, I told Rana that I'd been planning on selling as well and would like some advice on staging. I said that since kitchens and bathrooms didn't seem to leave as much room for creative exploration, I had a particular interest in her ideas about foyers and living rooms. I feigned fascination with the end table on which she kept her letters and asked if I could examine it while scanning the letters for her last name.

Taking my phone out on the pretense of finding a similar table online, I cyberstalked Rana and traced her workplace to the downtown core. I was beside myself because of the added insult it meant to Maisie, whose only exercise would be confined to the fenced-off, backyard-sized plots that heartless city planners think suffice as dog parks, and that she'd have to share with the other dogs of yuppie owners who would invariably be packed into the place like sardines. Did Rana stop for even a second to think about what this would do to Maisie? Could such a person be entrusted with the care of any dog, let alone one this exemplary? I put those questions aside to quell the ire they'd bring and asked to be led into the living room.

I expected the translocation of the dog bed would be a cinch, but Rana's constant supervision complicated things. I tried discreetly nudging it into place, but I pushed too far for me to be sure Maisie's face would be visible, and I couldn't try again without Rana taking notice. She was already annoyed by my self-invitation and seemed eager to get rid of me, but I pretended not to notice, remarking on everything in view and taking pictures from multiple angles; she got restless and excused herself to the bathroom, giving me the window I needed to move the bed and even affording me time to steal some kisses. Though I had no idea what the future would hold for us, for the next few nights, at least, I'd be able to see her; this bliss, however, came at the expense of my sleep, and in hindsight, I'm not sure this was a trade I should have made so readily.

Condo Life

After an uneventful week—the days spent devising ways to relieve Rana of walking duty, and the nights spent weeping while watching Maisie from afar—I noticed Chip's car pulling up and went out as if to check my mail, but in actuality, to investigate. He didn't leave his car but just honked and waited until Rana came out with Maisie in tow; she placed Maisie inside the car and kissed Chip, who then drove off. Rana would have walked in without noticing me had I not asked: "Finally grow tired of her?" She chuckled and shook her head, explaining that she needed to start packing that day and wanted Maisie out of her hair.

I offered her help not out of neighborly charity, but because I realized this could be a solution to the problem that had been nagging at me during the previous nights; I'd grown so accustomed to watching Maisie, and since I knew I couldn't peer into a condo with binoculars as easily as a house, I worried what might become of me if I was kept completely in the dark. It wasn't so much the loss of the joy of watching her that bothered me, but rather the frustration of having no clue as to how she was doing. Even though I planned to follow them on their walks, any insight into how she was doing would be skewed by the gleefulness she would exhibit whenever taken outside.

Somehow, I needed to get cameras inside the condo, and I realized I could do that by figuring out what she needed and implanting the cameras within housewarming presents. I volunteered to pack her favorite painting, making sure to break the frame so that I could insist on replacing it with one I'd purchase that would have a built-in camera to cover the living room. The kitchen, the bedroom, and the bathroom each suggested an item—a coffee maker, an alarm clock, and an automatic soap dispenser, respectively—that Rana could inadvertently put in spots that would render them useless, so to cover the entire house as well, I threw a robotic vacuum cleaner into the mix.

I purchased all the items, the nanny cams, and a soldering kit as soon as I left her, diverting the electricity needed to power the cameras from their power supplies before gift-wrapping them to present to her on the day of the move. To ensure that I'd be able to see the footage wherever I was, I installed a portable Wi-Fi hotspot device in the vacuum as well, to which I connected all the cameras for live streaming to my laptop and phone. For Maisie, I bought a new dog collar as a parting gift, which unbeknownst to Rana, had a GPS tracking chip that would—at least during the few days in which its battery lasted—help me establish their walking patterns.

I rented a car so as to trail Rana and the movers undetected and learn whatever I could about her building and her new neighborhood. Once there, I was able to find out her unit number by looking up recently closed listings at her building—information I didn't think I'd need but wanted to have—as well as how secure the building was; either from paranoia or unneighborliness, the condo's residents would make sure not to hold the door for anyone, which made entry difficult. I don't know why I was disappointed by this since I wasn't planning to enter, any more than I know why I thought up a potential workaround: going disguised as a food delivery man.

Chip had come over to help, so by nightfall, when he took Maisie out for a walk, unpacking was finished and all my cameras were in place. I followed them to a parkette, which—because of both its distance from the condo and its relative popularity with the city's heroin addict community—would certainly not be Rana's go-to route. When he returned, it appeared from the bedroom footage that he would be staying the night, which complicated my plans; if Chip were to walk Maisie in the morning, that would mean that twenty-four of the GPS collar's forty-eight to seventy-two hours of battery life would have been squandered without any useful data on Rana's walking preferences.

To draw him away, I drove to his house, where I planned to start a fire; I thought twice when I considered the ramifications of an arson investigation and chose instead to trigger his alarm by throwing a rock through a window. I'd barely returned to my car after doing so when I saw, on my live stream, Chip dressing frantically. He raced off and I drove back to the condo, where I spent the night waiting for Rana to take Maisie out. That moment came the next morning, and I followed them to the nearest park; its convenience and its superficial quaintness brought her back there at night, but since after sunset it became an outdoor bar and the center of the city's homeless nightlife, she went to another park, which became her default.

Things were going better than I had expected, since Maisie took a liking to the robotic vacuum and spent much of her days frolicking with it, allowing the camera to capture close-up shots from underneath her, but that was short-lived; the next time Chip came over, Rana, sensing his fear at living in his house after what he assumed to be a potential break-in, invited him to stay with her. He thanked her and declined, but when he excused himself to the bathroom and brooded, it occurred to me that the seed of doubt regarding Rana's sanity I had planted in his head was germinating, and he saw this offer as a warning; he left, citing sickness, and was markedly cooler toward Rana. Rana, sullen at the inexplicable chasm between them, spent hours in her room, presumably wondering what she'd done to mess things up; if she managed to muster the energy to take Maisie for a walk, it was usually to the nearest patch of greenery, beneath a tree at the entrance of her building.

Within days, the neglect of Maisie was noticeable; there was a mattedness in her fur, and her barks would quaver, trailing off in seconds to a whimper, which so pained me to hear that I considered scheduling an archery lesson to trick Chip into getting back with her again. I did no such thing though, knowing that while the pain that had turned Rana into a hermit was having such dire consequences on Maisie, and by extension, me, it was temporary, which wouldn't be the case for the barrier imposed by Chip's presence in her life.

But looking on idly became harder to do by the day. What good was the elimination of Chip from the picture if my Maisie were to die from Rana's lack of care? The walks had stopped altogether, and Maisie was defecating on the balcony; soon, full of pent-up energy, she took to tearing apart furniture while Rana was at work—unprecedented for her—which so incensed Rana that she started beating her. The cameras that I hoped would be masturbatory aides had become my windows into a campaign of neglect and abuse.

My horror was only matched by shame at my inaction, and soon, dognapping re-entered my mind. Since they were borne of concern for Maisie and indignation at her treatment, not just my desire for her, these thoughts were harder to set aside. In order to ensure both Maisie's survival and mine, I'd have to rescue her. Rana had no idea I knew where she lived, so I was confident that I wouldn't be a natural suspect if a dognapping was thought to have occurred, but there was still a chance of detection or capture. What was worse, I asked myself: to be known by the world as a zoophile, or to know myself to have turned a blind eye to the sufferings of my one true love? How selfish would it have been of me if after being saved by her, I failed to return the favor when she so needed me?

Dognapping

The most logical time for a break-in would be while Rana was at work, but although I'd gotten a sense of when Rana left, I was always too busy watching Maisie to see how long it took her to get there. To rectify this, I followed her for three days, after which I was confident that she'd take fifteen minutes to walk over, ten minutes longer than it would take me to drive back after confirming her entry. I bought and familiarized myself with a lock-picking set, and after snagging a job as a food delivery driver, which would give me both access to the condo and a bag in which I could sneak out a tranquilized Maisie, I felt I was ready to go.

Unfortunately, Rana left during what was a rather slow time of day, and because the security guards were away from the desk, presumably sleeping in a utility room, I had to wait a few minutes before a janitor noticed my loitering and opened the door for me. My heart nearly stopped when he said, "Isn't it a bit early for delivery?" But thankfully, he laughed and shook his head, adding, "These lazy millennials can't even make their own breakfasts." I chuckled along and sauntered to the elevator. Knowing that I had, at minimum, eight minutes and most likely, eight to eleven hours before Rana returned from work, I didn't worry too much; that is until, upon entering the door, I noticed that Rana had forgotten her work laptop.

There was no doubt that she recognized her mistake soon after arriving at her desk and was already on her way back; the only question was whether she'd taken a cab back home in an attempt to minimize time missed at work, which would mean she could walk in on me at any moment. I knew the best course of action would be to abort the plan, writing the entire thing off as a misadventure and escaping as quickly as possible, even if that meant I'd never see Maisie again; but before I could compel myself to leave, Maisie ran into the room and buried me with licks. Within seconds, I was stealing kisses and preparing the syringe.

She was too tired to be the playful girl I'd gotten used to, and she looked so downtrodden and relieved to see me that it almost made me cry to know I'd have to plunge a needle into her. I pulled away from one last deep kiss and did the deed; after she squirmed for a few seconds, I tucked her in the bag as gently as possible and left. One of Rana's neighbors was coming back to his apartment, so I was unable to lock the door, and was instead forced to say "Thanks again" to an empty apartment before calling the elevator; it came before he unlocked his door, and I had no choice but to step inside.

I sent it up a floor, planning to pop back down and lock Rana's door once the neighbor was gone, but when I reached Rana's floor, the elevator next to mine opened as well, and she stepped out, gasping. I hid as best I could against the wall of the elevator, too afraid of being noticed to reach for the *Close Door* button; by the time it closed on its own, she was frantically calling out for Maisie. I knew that if she called the police, due to the area's high property values, they wouldn't be far off, so remaining calm was of the utmost importance; I tried every breathing exercise I could before saying farewell to the janitor and heading for the bike I'd locked outside.

The sound of sirens had always been a comfort to me, a reassurance that the authorities had more urgent concerns than whatever petty crime I'd have been committing at the moment, but when I heard them now, I was so sure they were for me that they drowned out all other sounds and even thoughts. I had parked my getaway car a block away, but it was in the direction of the sirens, and I didn't know if I should go straight for it or lap around; I decided to go for it so as to seem as if I had nothing to worry about.

As I neared the intersection, an ambulance zipped through, and I was so relieved to know that it was only someone having a medical emergency that I couldn't hear the horn of the car I was cutting off when I made a turn; the driver slowed, but not soon enough to miss me entirely, and he clipped my rear wheel, throwing me off the bike. He jumped out to see how I was, but when I stood myself up, he turned back to his car to assess the damage; I was inside my car by the time he looked at me again, and I almost ran him over when he tried to block my escape, ostensibly to force me to pay his repair bill. I was worried he might have gotten my license plate, but that wasn't the most pressing matter at hand; Maisie was silent and motionless, and I wondered if that was because of the tranquilizer or because she was dead.

Even as I drove, I couldn't take my eyes off the bag, except when a horn alerted me that I was veering through lanes or a scream told me that I was blowing through a crosswalk. I pulled over to the shoulder of the road, but I was too afraid to open the bag in public, being concerned about the police's arrival, so I nudged her at first. "Maisie, are you awake?" Nothing. "Maisie, stop playing around. Say something!" My voice cracked. "Speak, Maisie, speak!" But to no avail; I wept uncontrollably.

Then there was a slight stir in the bag, and I thought I heard a groan. Squinting through one eye, I slowly opened the zipper, and there wasn't so much as a scratch on her. I took her out and pressed my ear to her chest, and—at least until the sound of mine drowned it out—I could hear her heartbeat. I burst out of the car, spinning around with her in my arms, screaming to anyone who could hear, "She's alive! Maisie's alive!"

The commotion woke her up entirely, and when she licked me, I was so overwrought that I started kissing her, right there in the middle of the road. I heard the cars honking in protest, but I sat down anyway and made out with her, thrilled that she was finally mine. Some men had the temerity to try to separate us, but I held on, vowing never to let go of her. They backed off when I snarled and watched with disgust until a police cruiser drove by, which they waved over.

The arrival of the cops reminded me of my crime, and I snapped out of my romantic bliss and tried to act unthreatening; I put Maisie down, told her to stay, and walked over, but noticing their apprehension and the hand of one of the officers inching toward his pistol, I stopped. I thought I'd introduce some levity—"Didn't mean to hold up traffic, officers!"—but they were a tough crowd.

One of them engaged me in conversation, mostly asking about Maisie; I told her she was mine, and that we just had a little scare. I tried to break away from the conversation and head home with her, but his tone changed slightly. "We're just going to wait for the ambulance, okay?"

"Ambulance?" I didn't notice sustaining any injuries during the crash, but I assumed my adrenaline just kept me from feeling them, so I checked my clothes in case; they were covered in blood. I looked all over for a cut, but I couldn't find anything until I happened to glance at Maisie: she was a crushed and bloody mess. When I saw her snout, which the force of the crash had caved in, I ran over, desperate to comfort her, but I was restrained by the police. Unmoved by my agony, they placed me in handcuffs. The cop didn't know how right he was when he said, "They're for your own protection," because if my hands were free, I'd have torn my eyes out rather than continue to see Maisie like that. I passed out instead.

Recovery

I awoke to find myself in a psychiatric hospital, but how I got there, how long I was to be confined, and on what grounds I was being held were all a mystery to me. I racked my mind, but all that came to it were memories of the dream I'd just awoken from. I was an assistant in what appeared to be an operating room. Men and women, dressed in smocks and masks, like me, were huddled around a table on which lay a figure covered by a white shroud. I asked the person closest to me if we were performing a surgery; she shook her head, and said "A *pawtopsy*," before pulling off the sheet, revealing Maisie's bloody corpse.

The same horror that woke me came back upon recalling the dream, and I cried, drawing the attention of a nearby nurse. She entered with trepidation but appeared to be pleasantly surprised by my demeanor; I wondered what it was that she'd gotten used to, from which mere lucidity was such a departure. More importantly, what did they know about Maisie and me? I noticed that although somewhat reassured, she was still uneasy—it seemed that this state of mine, unfamiliar to her as it was to me, was to be thought of as unpredictable, though an improvement over whatever they had to deal with since my admission—so, desperate to say anything but at a loss, I said, "Good morning."

"Good morning, Mr. Bogdan," she said timidly. "How are you feeling?"

"Sad." There seemed no reason to lie, but I regretted my candidness immediately—since, not knowing what I was being held for or what diagnoses the doctors were pondering, I wasn't sure if misspeaking could get me locked up for life; until I knew my situation, it'd be best to stay mum. Before she could reassure me, I added, as a way of making inroads with her, "Please, call me John."

"Well, John, do you want to get ready for breakfast?" Eating was the last thing on my mind, but fearing that a refusal would be another symptom on my chart, I agreed. The urge to demand an audience with the doctors was hard to suppress and would likely have been impossible if I didn't fear that an eagerness to leave might cause more suspicion. She provided me with toiletries and escorted me to the restroom adjoining my room.

I tried to avoid my eyes in the mirror—scared off by the bags that had grown under them—but I'm not sure they could have been worse to look at than the rest of my face; my gauntness and disgusting beard were almost beautiful when compared to what my teeth had become after weeks without brushing. I wouldn't be able to do anything about the beard until they would trust me with a razor—at this point, I wasn't allowed shoelaces—so I decided to do the best

I could with the teeth. The nurse heard my groaning, the result of a cavity, and provided me with a more delicate toothpaste while assuring me she'd see to it that I saw a dentist; I remembered I hadn't asked her name, and, after finding out it was Jess, I told her how touched I was by her kindness.

My appreciation of Jess didn't beget a trust for the institution, however, and I returned to the task of having myself released. There was no doubt they knew I was found making out with a dead dog, but the lack of handcuffs and police supervision led me to believe that Rana hadn't made Maisie's disappearance known to the authorities, perhaps thinking her disappearance a deliverance; I cursed her heartlessness, wondering how differently this could have played out if Maisie had been mine from the start, but I couldn't do so too vigorously, as it so benefited me in my present condition—I could say Maisie was mine and prevent my obsession and criminality from ending up on my chart. What seemed harder to explain was why the death of one's dog would have been so impactful as to bring about a nervous breakdown; I wasn't able to come up with a fix before I was joined by a team of doctors.

I froze, hoping they hadn't seen my pacing or heard my agitated mumbling, but they casually greeted me, which assured me they hadn't. The one who did the most talking, Dr. Wu, elicited a feeling of familiarity, although I couldn't recall ever meeting him, and that, coupled with the same look as Jess's—

a seeming recognition of and delight in a change in me—made me suspect we'd spoken since I was admitted; the others, because of their youth and wine-stained lips, were, I assumed, residents, so I paid no attention to controlling their perception of me. After answering some mundane questions about how I felt upon waking—each as normally as I could—Dr. Wu, changing his tone to something almost guarded, said: "You seemed like you were doing a lot of thinking when we came in. Mind if I ask what you were thinking about?"

I chuckled and shook my head in amusement—calculated to put them off guard, and apparently, successful at doing so. "I've been telling myself for a while that I wouldn't need to come here, but I guess I was wrong." A little more chuckling before a sigh: "Hopefully, it's for the best."

"I'm sure it will be, John. How long did you think you'd end up here?"

With that I saw my ticket: I could distract from my zoophilia by emphasizing my many other potential mental illnesses. I told them about the existential crisis I was undergoing when I met Maisie. Hiding my excitement upon registering their fascination was challenging since I knew I had them on the hook, but fortunately, it was interrupted before it could show when Dr. Wu asked me who Maisie was. I was taken aback—I knew Maisie's name wasn't on her collar, and it made no sense that he could know it unless Rana had reported the dognapping after all and the police had shared that information with him—but he mentioned I'd been saying the name almost constantly since my arrival.

There was no way to be sure I wasn't making loving pronouncements when they heard me mention her name, so I was hesitant to say she was a dog, and instead I tried to invent a human female character with the same name. But when Dr. Wu reiterated his question, all I could say to keep from seeming evasive was, "She's a dog," before clarifying with, "my dog." When I reviewed the statement in my mind to reassure myself there wasn't anything in it they'd think strange, the tense stuck out—she isn't anything anymore.

"What's wrong?" Dr. Wu asked, noticing the trembling of my lip and my welling tears.

"She's dead." I tried to keep from remembering my last moments with her by shifting my mind to the more pleasant parts of our time together, like our make-out sessions, but that brought to mind the fact I'd been making out with her corpse; this hit me with such a blow that I audibly groaned, prompting a fit of furious note-scribbling by the residents. I was so disgusted I tried scraping my tongue with my teeth to get any trace of her off it, but it wasn't enough, and I took to scratching at it; thankfully, the doctors restrained and sedated me before I ripped it out altogether.

The next thing I remember is being woken up by the sound of a thud; I turned so fast I nearly fell out of my bed, but it was just Jess, who had accidentally knocked over a chair as she was checking on me. It was nice to see her, but I wasn't in the talking mood, so I responded to her apology with the politest grunt I could muster and rolled over to fake sleep. I was in such a haze I worried they had lobotomized me, so once Jess left, I ran my hands over my head in search for any stitches; not finding any wasn't a relief, however, since it I knew it could only mean I was drugged.

I desperately tried to remember being medicated, but even though I did recall being tied to a bed, and the doctors inundating me with questions—my name, my age, etc.—until I tried to break free and was sedated, I wasn't sure whether this was a memory or a confabulation; I leaned toward thinking it valid when other similar ones emerged, where I'd wake up to different, yet equally simple questions, and of being put under once I panicked. Although I couldn't discern any order to the memories, I felt as if there was some progression, as if their questions were becoming increasingly penetrating, until finally, I remembered them asking who Maisie was.

I knew how they'd respond to the real answer—*She's my one true love*—with as much certainty as I knew that said response spoke not to a fault in me or my affection but the society that would condemn them both, but I wondered how I could ever lie my way out of the hospital so that I could evangelize zoophilia if Maisie's mere mention was so painful that it debilitated me. Sharing my thoughts was the obvious solution to mitigating the pain they brought, but doing so without triggering their *homospecistic* bias would require some deception, and I couldn't think of a lie I was sure wouldn't blow up in my face and cause me to be labeled a hostile patient. The doctors entered before I had time to formulate a game plan, so I responded to their questions by leaning on the truth as much as possible.

"She was my dog, but she's dead now."

"I'm so sorry, John. My dog died a couple of years ago, and I know it's hard."

"No, you don't!" I blurted before catching myself and reverting to sadness. "She was all I had."

I looked up, expecting sympathy, but instead, I saw apprehension in the eyes of the residents, all of them too enthralled to take notes, and a look of what I can only assume was gentle disapproval from Dr. Wu. To alleviate my confusion, he explained that even though it might have felt like Maisie was a lone bright spot in my life, there were, in fact, others available to me—and most everyone else— that he would help me learn to tap into. Hitherto, I'd assumed any man who spent as much time on his hair as Dr. Wu did would be vacuous, but I couldn't help but agree; my insistence on relying solely on Maisie had set me up for a collapse.

I teared up, but the doctors seemed to think it an appropriate response to the digestion of such information and did nothing to stop me. Once my bout of crying passed, ambivalent with curiosity and cynicism, I asked, "What else is there?"

"Well, for starters, John, you'll have to learn to take care of yourself a little bit better."

I nodded knowingly. "Sleep."

"Yes, sleep is vital; you hadn't been getting any. Food, too. John, you've got to remember to slow down and take care of your physical needs." He was right again; I'd mistakenly thought that Maisie's love elevated me past the physical plane of existence, and by extension, past its considerations, but I could see where that had landed me.

Despite my agreement in principle, I could think of no realistic way to implement the suggestion; it wasn't that these things diminished in importance—I'm sure I'd have been able to expound upon the necessity of sleep if questioned—it's that they seemed trivial when my life was falling apart, which is what it felt like at the time. I didn't press that point with him, because allowing my love—and my desire to preserve it—to have gotten that far was, I readily admitted to myself, insane, and I was in no position to argue.

They explained to me the medication I'd been given and armed me with some breathing techniques, which they said would help when I sensed myself agitated; I nodded silently throughout, which gave Dr. Wu enough confidence in my compliance to give me the first bits of information I had about my internment: I'd tried to jump off an overpass after

Maisie died. The attempt meant I was to be held for at least seventy-two hours, but the tongue-ripping incident meant that the holding period was to be extended until they believed I was no longer a harm to myself.

"Harm to myself?" I thought once they left. "What about Maisie?" Yes, the immediate cause had been the impact from the car, but she wouldn't have been in its way if I hadn't put her there. I thought it was love that clouded my thinking, but I knew the same word—love—couldn't be used to describe both her feelings for me, which reintroduced me to life, and my feelings for her, which tore it away; mine was merely an obsession, and a fatal one at that. I struggled to figure out what the difference was before their nepenthe kicked in.

What I meant when I said I loved her was that she had elicited an emotion from me, which because of its pleasance and novelty, I assumed to be the real thing; however, it soon became clear to me that it wasn't a single emotion she had stirred within me, and that not only had I falsely combined them under the umbrella of love, I'd blotted out the negatives. Had I taken into consideration, for instance, the terror that had gripped me when I'd contemplate separation from her, I might have checked myself before I tried to abduct her. I felt almost glad to be confined in this hospital, where I'd have time to think things through.

The nature of my depravity initially seemed multifarious, but in thinking about my many seeming deficits, I realized that they were symptoms of a deeper lacking: an inability or unwillingness to consider the impact of our relationship on Maisie. Because I had never intellectualized this idea, I wasn't bothered by what obtaining her might have implied, let alone the perversity of the desire itself. I had been blinded by how much I had riding on our connection. Her acceptance of me had been the only assurance I had that I was of value, and because of this, not having her affection would have meant not having a positive conception of myself; without her, I was nothing. Any serious consideration of her feelings or the negative effects my actions might have had on her, which true love would have brought, was necessarily impossible; it wasn't about her, it was about me and my sense of adequacy, so I had readily accepted the assumption that whatever I was feeling was shared.

Until such a time when I was able to develop a firmer sense of self, I wouldn't be in a frame of mind conducive to true love, and even if I was lucky enough to come across another as amazing as Maisie, I'd squander that opportunity like I squandered this one. Despite the despair, I knew at least that I had something to work toward, which seemed like it would be enough to keep me going for the duration of my hospitalization.

Following a vague notion that the opposite of obsession is simple appreciation, I tried to train myself to default to the latter by thinking about the person nearest me, Jess, who'd just entered. Here was a bright, beautiful young woman, who—although it was her job to care for me—did so with a degree of consideration and delicacy that was above and beyond; I apologized for any trouble I'd caused her since I'd been admitted and thanked her again for her attentiveness. She seemed genuinely touched and assured me that I was a great patient before adding, "We all care about you, John." It was a lie, but a lie that spoke to such a beautiful worldview I couldn't censure it.

Jess told me there was something about to happen in the common area she thought would cheer me up. Confused, I followed her to a room where several other patients had assembled. I was hesitant to mingle with these folks despite being in the same boat as them, so I decided to keep my distance and focus on plotting my deception of the staff. But then I noticed a gaggle of patients huddled in a circle, and their cooing and giggling sparked my curiosity; thus, I pushed my way through the crowd and found that the commotion was over a litter of puppies that the patients were taking turns playing with. To my more priggish readers, I say relax—I'm a zoophile, not a pedophile; though this sight brought me delight, it was only because of the joy, excitement, and ease of mind I saw them bring to my fellow patients.

I was reminded of my discovery of the serenity that comes with vicarious joy, and I resolved to return to the path I'd diverged from after I started obsessing, hoping it would be the key to the emotional stability I knew I'd need for a healthy relationship; even though I was eager to play with the puppies myself—again, with no pedo-zoophilic intentions—I wasn't entirely disappointed when the orderlies had to take them away. I passed up my turn to play with them, not out of any fear of arousal but so that the others could have a bit more time. I felt for the first time since the night of my epiphany in the bar restroom that I was adding to the sum total of human happiness, at least until I was led back to my room for the night and the gloominess re-emerged.

I was too caught up rehashing my conversation with the doctors to pay attention to the effects of the medication, so after Jess gave me my evening meds and left me alone for the night, I stayed vigilant for any changes in my thought processes; most importantly, I wanted to know if my feelings for Maisie persisted once medicated. I lay there, waiting for the introduction of a voice of reason that would talk me out of my feelings, but all that I noticed was a dullness coming over me, as if my mind was slipping away with nothing taking its place. Ideas would form but seemed to dissipate whenever I'd pursue them; only the recognition of the absence of thought and the muted fear that came with it seemed to persist.

Upon waking, I frantically devised tests to assess my mental faculties; after successfully recalling the names of state capitals and a couple of poems, I was convinced the dulling effect was only temporary. I assured myself that the doctors couldn't force me to take the medication once I was out of the hospital; the surest way to minimize my intake would be to appear open to their treatments. I shifted attention to Maisie, hoping to lose myself in happy thoughts while I still could, but the specter of my next dosage was too overwhelming.

I knew I would lack the creativity needed to produce a convincing story of a breakdown while on these meds and that I'd only be believed if I relayed my own, but fearing that they'd conflate my zoophilia with psychosis and try to medicate away my one source of happiness, I thought I needed a way to keep them from getting hung up on it. I decided that substituting a human woman wouldn't adequately explain the shame and confusion I'd felt upon discovering my attraction, so I used a man; my zoophilia became allegorical bisexuality, and my Maisie became Miles.

When it came time to speak to Dr. Wu, one-on-one, my mind was so sapped by the drugs that I found it hard to relay anything of importance; of my epiphany, I could only muster, "It was life-changing," to which he nodded, sparing me the look of condescension I'd have given anyone who'd said something of the like to me. When he asked me to elaborate, the things that seemed to have followed so naturally before were lost to me entirely; all I had were granules of my philosophy, which my attempts to articulate made into disjointed ramblings. "I'd only ever thought of myself; how I could be happy, you know? But then, I ... I'd—" My impulse was to pull at my hair, so frustrated was I by my ineloquence, but I used the breathing techniques instead. He seemed pleased to see me employing them and took notes while I wondered how manipulation had become so second nature to me that I was able to do it even while in this state.

"Once I found out I had the ability to make people feel better and how much better it made me feel, I thought I had to devote my life to it."

"Is that why you left your job—because everything else seemed unimportant?"

"Yes!" I almost sprang from my chair. Feeling understood rather than scrutinized filled me with such excitement—I can only compare the feeling to that of a vagrant who, roaming city streets in search of cigarette butts, finds an unopened pack—that I allowed myself to think my discharge was imminent. "You see now, right?"

"A bit, but those other things—like your job— they're important too, aren't they?"

He got me. "Just like sleep, right?"

"That's right, John. I think you're onto something when you say that we should work toward improving the lives of others, but you should take some time and think things through so you can communicate your ideas more effectively."

I knew I was jumping from A to Z, but I didn't know how to tell him that B to Y were in there as well, even though I couldn't access them; doing so, I was afraid, would reveal my antipathy toward the medication. Saying nothing seemed the wisest course of action, but embarrassment prompted me to excuse myself.

"I'm just feeling a bit of fogginess is all." I cursed myself inwardly for having mentioned it, but to my surprise, Dr. Wu seemed sympathetic and assured me that we'd figure out a medication regimen that would eliminate or at least minimize any side effects.

Doing so took a few weeks, in which time my progression had made such an impact on Dr. Wu that he was confident I was no longer in need of such intensive care, and I was transferred to an outpatient program. It came as a shock to me, since I didn't notice any fundamental differences in my thought processes, just an abatement of the stress I was under, but as you might imagine, I had no compulsion to mention this; I thanked them for the help and got home as soon as possible to build a new life for myself.

Employment seemed like a fitting place to start. It was the belief of my new doctor that adjusting to a new career would be an unnecessary addition of stress at this crucial juncture in my life, so she instead encouraged me to go back to my old firm. She explained to the HR department that in terminating me for my outburst, they were demonstrating a criminal lack of willingness to accommodate employees with mental illness, and I was reinstated, much to the chagrin of my managing director.

His subconscious distrust of the mentally ill and the resultant lack of tasks assigned to me meant I was contributing less to the firm than a mailroom intern, and although this felt insulting, I didn't protest; my lingering sense of intellectual enfeeblement, magnified by the use of psychiatric medications, led me to agree. The sense that anyone else would have been fired and the knowledge I was being held to a lower standard than other employees had a diminishing effect on my self-worth, but it paled in comparison with the effect created by my co-workers.

I was assured by HR that my illness wouldn't be discussed with my co-workers, but the changing relations I noticed made me suspect someone had divulged my secret. I'd grown used to engaging in either witty or flirty banter, but now, even when I spoke about something strictly work-related, I noticed mixed fear and disgust—as well as a desire to escape—on the part of my interlocutors, as if I were contagious. My doctor said withdrawal wasn't the answer, but these interactions were so painful to me and seemingly burdensome to everyone else that I couldn't help but keep to myself.

It was easier with my friends, at least the ones who would even respond to my attempts to reach out. As with the doctors, I left only the zoophilia out while telling them what had happened, and although they admitted to being unable to understand, they told me they didn't need to, which helped tremendously. Despite this, and even though they were willing to learn about and accommodate my condition, their ignorance coupled with my inability to articulate thoughts led to repeated breakdowns in communication, leaving us all frustrated. Of course, whenever I'd bail on an outing at the last minute, they'd admonish me for undermining their attempts to make me feel better, and it didn't help that in these moments, I sensed contempt from them, as if I should be grateful for their continued presence in my life; soon, their company began to feel more isolating than anything.

My doctor assured me that I should feel proud. I'd overcome a great deal, and simply getting out of bed, showing up to work, and going through the motions of life required a lot of courage and strength on my part. Unfortunately, these pep talks of hers were counterproductive, because not only did having my mundane actions applauded make me feel like a toddler undergoing potty training, they made clear to me the gulf between the way I should feel and the way I actually felt, which was doubly depressing. Worse still was the fear—intensifying with every alteration of my medication and with each barely avoided panic attack—that mine was a depression incurable by modern medicine. I was, in a word, rudderless, and although I never mentioned it to my doctor, I began contemplating suicide yet again.

It was from sheer desperation that I began to think of how I could rekindle the feelings Maisie brought; without them, I assumed, my life would be at best a grind for which, as the return of my suicidal ideations proved, I was temperamentally underequipped. Experiencing it again, I hoped, would prove to me that I was still capable of feeling it, as well as giving me a reservoir of happy memories I could use to convince myself life wasn't all bad, since those of Maisie herself were still too painful to revisit.

The following Saturday marked the beginning of the Iditarod, an annual dogsled race in Alaska, during which I was all but guaranteed to meet a specimen as fine as Maisie. I voiced my concerns to the doctor, careful to avoid mentioning anything that might trigger another involuntary commitment, and was convincing enough that she beseeched my employer to accept my abrupt vacation request.

A Far Distant Place

I made a point of coming late to the race's ceremonial start for fear that the officials might easily detect any flashes of emotion if I was standing at the very forefront of the crowd, but with each team that was introduced, I noticed, in place of the inappropriate arousal I expected, a heightening despair; I'd look upon each dog, scanning it and my thoughts in response to it, until noticing an absence of the joy I had felt from Maisie, I'd give up on it and move to another. The cycle of apprehension and sorrow seemed to be broken when I saw a dog so reminiscent of my Maisie that I unwittingly began pushing through the crowd to get a closer look; seeing its eyes, however, the heterochromatism of which was nothing if not eerie, was so disconcerting that even if I hadn't been accosted by the father of a child whom I'd inadvertently shoved to the ground, I'd have left to keep from crying in public.

I went straight to the nearest bar, despite my doctor's repeated warnings about mixing alcohol and my medication, planning to drink myself into a stupor deep enough to keep me from removing the plastic bag I planned to asphyxiate myself with.

Though the images my mind conjured of a desperate struggle for air were harrowing, my resolve never waned, as both the alcohol and the memories of Maisie's corpse were effective in driving away any desire to live I still had. It would have been perfect had my focus not been broken by the arrival of a woman who sat beside me at the bar.

Her presence was so oppressive to me that though my drink was finished, I opted to wait in silence until the bartender noticed my empty glass rather than waving him over, which would have required turning in the woman's direction and risking being dragged into a conversation. To pass the time and to keep the social anxiety I'd felt since her approach from boiling over, I tried distracting myself by looking at everything in view; I settled on the mirror behind the bar, a bad choice, since focusing on my face—particularly my red, puffy eyes—only made my anguish more pointed. Afraid of breaking down and being cut off by the bartender, I averted my gaze, inadvertently glancing at her face; we made eye contact through the mirror. I panicked, turning to the opposite side so quickly, I almost knocked over my drink.

I took so long deciphering the expression she had—which I'd concluded must have been pity—that I didn't even recognize the approach of the bartender until after he'd taken her order and left. My consternation was more a result of knowing myself to be sullying this woman's experience than anger at my inability to hide my emotions, and since her reaction to my anguish had given me such a positive impression of her—that of an observant, kind person—I set to undo the damage and struck up a conversation so as to seem normal. But when my inquiry into the quality of her evening was thrown back at me and my response was deemed "not very convincing," even the light hearted way in which she said it wasn't enough to keep me from sliding back into despair.

Said despair, however, wasn't complete, as it was checked by a sense of awe regarding her perceptiveness and the resultant desire to unburden myself; though I wanted to tell her everything, I wasn't able to say anything more than "my dog" before stammering, too desperate to keep from being overwrought by my crescendoing emotion to speak. Sheer embarrassment had always been enough to keep me from expressing any such feelings publicly before, but since her expression—anguish that seemed to mirror mine—made it clear that my attempts at concealment weren't working, I gave in and wept. Before I managed to stop, she'd led me to another table, where I could cry uninhibited by the bartender and other inquisitive patrons; she was even thoughtful enough to have furnished me with tissues and some water.

Once I'd collected myself, although I wanted to continue with my explanation, her saying, "It's okay, we don't have to talk about it," put an end to that;

still desirous to keep from being a complete buzzkill, I prodded her to talk in my stead, hoping she'd get caught up enough in making conversation to forget my morosity. Fearful of mentioning the race lest I remember Maisie and bawl again, I spoke instead of Anchorage; unbeknownst to me, it was her hometown, and since her family had moved there because of her father's career as a musher, talk of huskies was all but unavoidable.

She realized, by the turn in my mood, that the reminder wasn't welcome and apologized for having mentioned dogs. Sensing that a shift back to small talk would have seemed too unnatural, she ventured, with trepidation, to address the state I was in. "By the time we were teenagers, my dad couldn't force us to come to the races with him, but once he died, we thought going would be a nice way to honor his memory. That first year— "she trailed off, adding only that it "was rough" before assuring me, after a sudden shift in mood, that the race had become a highlight of her year. The only thing I could wish for at that moment more than being the type of person capable of having their mood elevated so easily was that she hadn't said anything at all; added to the brooding over my life were bitter thoughts directed toward a woman who, despite my seeing as vapid, had only inadvertently displayed said vapidity to me in an earnest attempt to lift my spirits.

Not trusting myself enough to venture a reply that wasn't a vitriolic dismissal, I sighed and tried to get the attention of a server. I couldn't bring myself to look at her until I heard her standing up to excuse herself to the restroom, and from what seemed like dourness on her face, I gathered that it was a ruse to divest herself of this downer; I alternated between self-chastisement, commending her for her intuitiveness in distancing herself from me, and worrying about having sent her into a depression by undermining whatever her coping strategies were, but that all ended when she returned to her seat, looking unperturbed, and I was forced to confront the fact that I'd grossly exaggerated my impact on her.

She asked if a server had come during her absence, and when I said none had, she waved one down herself. Though she seemed to want to move to a discussion of the menu items, I felt I'd be remiss if I left her statement unaddressed, and having admitted to myself the slight irrationality of an outright dismissal of a worldview I'd only had a sentence worth of insight into, I thought it fitting to inquire further: "So, what changed?"

She was deep in thought, pondering, I assumed, the amount of insanity required to levy a question that bespoke familiarity toward an acquaintance of ten minutes, but I knew that to be my second faulty assumption about her once she began explaining that although the memories of her father, which made the first trip so jarring, still came to her, the accompanying pain no longer did; it wasn't easy to hold back the immediate follow-up that came to mind— "So, you just don't care about him anymore?" It might seem like a harsh thing to think, but you have to understand that at the time, my thoughts of Maisie seemed to serve only as reminders of her absence, and to react to them with anything other than sadness seemed to be a callous disservice; the egotism and irrationality of the reverse implication— that my brooding was somehow a kindness—hadn't occured to me just yet.

Thankfully, she continued before I gave voice to any of the abhorrent ideas circling my head, explaining that she'd realized that in dwelling on the fact of her father's death, she'd been ruining all the pleasant memories, without which her mental image of her father was just a ghoulish caricature; not only was her newer, circumspect manner of thinking about him more in line with reality, but it had the added benefit of being "what he would have wanted."

If there was something to all of this, I wondered, it meant I wouldn't have to find a new Maisie; I could keep her and my feelings for her enshrined in my mind and still learn to feel new things for new lovers, be they human or canine. Curious to see what this type of reminiscing looked like, I asked her if she'd mind sharing one of her memories. Unfortunately, I am restricted to retelling only that which I'd paid full attention to, and I cannot accurately transcribe her story in a way that wouldn't be uselessly broad—that it was about her father's lead dog and her relationship to it—but my inattentiveness wasn't a result of ignoring her, but a sign of how transported I was by seeing her so happy, as well as the shock, whenever she'd glance over and find me staring at her, that it wasn't diminished by my presence in the least.

Though I managed to coax her into telling a few more anecdotes, my fear that the burden of conversation would inevitably be thrust upon me was confirmed when slightly abashed at talking about herself for so long, she prompted me to tell her a bit about myself. I was flustered, afraid that by talking I'd reveal to her the disordered workings of my mind, which I was sure would bring about the end of our conversation, but the opportunely timed arrival of the waitress saved me from that, though my relief was short-lived.

The waitress, it seems, was informed of my emotional outburst by the bartender, so when my interlocutor ordered us two drinks, the waitress politely explained that she couldn't serve me and offered to bring over just one. I was fine with this, as I'd begun feeling light-headed during the last few drinks and had no intention of drinking more; however, my new friend was offended on my behalf and insisted on taking me to another bar with more accommodating staff.

I tried to reject the offer, desperate to return to my hotel room before my condition deteriorated further, but she was too indignant to listen. Within a few paces, I began to sense myself tipping over to my right, and the act of walking itself took up all my focus. In my panic to readjust, I went too far the other way, barely keeping myself from plunging into the road by grabbing hold of a parking meter. She thought my umming, the closest to screaming for help I could muster in that state, was due to not knowing how to address her, as we hadn't yet introduced ourselves and turned to do just that; I distinctly remember her turning around to tell me her name was Lacie and hurrying over to ask if I was all right. After that I just have a scattered memory, possibly a confabulation, of her picking my head up off the ground, frantically urging me to keep me awake as she called the paramedics on her phone with blood-stained hands. The next thing I knew, I was waking up in another hospital bed.

This time, however, she was asleep in a chair beside me, at least until my groaning—a result of the pain from the teeth I'd chipped in my fall—woke her. Noticing my confusion upon seeing her, she said, "I didn't want you waking up alone, so I just told them I was your girlfriend. I hope you don't mind."

I shook my head, unable to speak for worry she'd found out about my condition. Her concern at my silence forced me to say something, so with trepidation, I asked, "What did they say?"

"They said you should have known better than to mix your meds with booze."

Though she said this with friendly delicacy, I couldn't bring myself to look at her; to remove from her the burden of babysitting me, I said, "I really appreciate what you did, but you don't have to stay," before adding, upon remembering that the race's official restart was only a few hours away, "I wouldn't want you missing the action on my account."

In fits and starts, which I attributed at first to a discomfort at being in my presence, she said "Actually, I was thinking, since they said you weren't going to stay long, that maybe—if you want, of course—you could see it with me. My brother and sister will be there, and I'm sure they'd enjoy the extra company." I still thought myself an encumbrance, but moved to excitement by the shock of being wanted, I agreed immediately.

She stayed with me until I was released, which—due to the influx of injured drunken tourists—was some time. Sure that she wouldn't have been informed as to the nature of my illness, and concerned that if kept in the dark during our trip, she'd be on edge throughout, I proceeded to tell her about my medication, the reason I was on it, and a brief history of my time since being discharged from the psychiatric hospital; at times, shocked at how open I was being, I would peek at her, certain I'd find an empty chair, but she stayed put, and for the first time since my internment in the psychiatric hospital, I felt as if I could say whatever was on the top of my mind. By the time I'd explained my theory of benign douchebaggery, I could look into her eyes without any fear of judgment, although I had to cut those gazes short lest I lose my train of thought while admiring them.

Though I was too enthralled to note the passage of time, it occurred to me once I was discharged that I'd missed the bus I was planning to take to nearby Willow, where the race would officially start. Lacie offered to drive me, and I accepted, not knowing until we arrived at her house that she meant for us to go by snowmobile, as is customary for the locals; I resisted but soon relented, if for no other reason than the worry that in arguing over the chances of finding parking near the starting line, we might miss the event altogether.

She gave me my own snowmobile, but too afraid to drive it, I accepted instead an offer to ride with her. The height difference was such that my bent knees constricted the movement of her arms, and even though she said that wouldn't be a problem, I went most of the distance with my eyes closed for fear that I would convulse in panic, throw off her steering, and tip us over. To make matters worse, the sting caused by the cold wind blowing against the exposed nerves of my teeth was only mitigated by tucking my upper lip around them, which I couldn't do while speaking; rather than condemning Lacie to an awkward, silent ride, I tried to make conversation, barely able to keep the pain from revealing itself in my voice.

Once there, I was given a cold welcome by her older sister, Laura, which only worsened once Lacie had explained that we'd met at a bar the night before; however, that was more than made up for by her younger brother Kevin's congeniality. Laura's disdain for me was soon mutual, as her bloviating drowned out both the announcers and interrupted Lacie's, Kevin's, and my attempts at conversing, but thankfully my interactions with Quincey's owner had taught me to feign attentiveness, which in addition to the gift of my share of the snow-cooled beers, served to ingratiate me to her enough that I was spared the insults she intermittently hurled at her siblings. Unfortunately, dealing with her required so much attention that I wasn't able to get to know Lacie any better that afternoon, and when she told me that she had no intention of following the race any further, the trip to Nome being too expensive for them to justify, I was nearly thrown into a panic.

Inviting her to join me alone, I thought, could either be interpreted as too forward or downright creepy, but I was so unwilling to say goodbye so soon that I extended the offer to all three of them. Kevin couldn't afford to take time off work, but once the others agreed, I called the travel agency, reserving the seats of a couple that had recently dropped out. Our days were thoroughly planned out for us, and the fact that meals were shared meant that I'd have little time alone with Lacie during the trip, but Laura's drinking, I hoped, would give me enough time at night to eke out some alone time. I'd gotten a sense that she'd had a problem at Willow and had brought a suitcase of booze to ensure she wouldn't have a sober moment.

As I was new to all this, nothing about the arrival of the first team struck me as odd, other than the fury of the musher, despite being in the lead; it wasn't until Lacie pointed out the sled's rightward veer that I noticed one of the dogs was limping and trailing blood behind it. When they pulled in, the musher took a bootie off the injured dog's limp paw, revealing a weak, yet pulsating stream of blood. The vet ran over to attend to the wound, which she explained was caused by stepping on a shard of ice, the undoing of many a sled dog.

I watched the operation, like the others, with bated breath until I saw Lacie, who was staring at the musher, scowling; he was pacing, looking only at his watch or the horizon, and when another team came into view, he turned to the vet, ordering her to move to the next dog. Neither the vet's concerns about the pain the dog was in nor the murmuring of the onlookers were enough to distract him from the time he'd lose in being one dog down for the remainder of the race; he told her she could do whatever she wanted with it once he was gone, and in our collective pusillanimity, we said nothing. Though the musher seemed pleased with himself at causing her acquiescence, that waned once he realized he was the subject of a cell phone recording, and he lunged, precipitating a struggle to destroy the device.

Entertaining though that commotion was, I couldn't watch both it and Lacie, who under the guidance of the vet, was doing her best to care for the injured dog; I tried to help, but she'd already managed to stem the bleeding. There was enough time after the departure of the musher and before the arrival of the next team for the vet to do a proper assessment, during which she discovered that the dog had already lost too much blood to last long without a transfusion; since there wasn't a nearby animal hospital, she recommended euthanasia. Lacie nodded, and the vet stepped aside to get the necessary supplies.

The sight itself was pitiful enough, moving everyone present to the verge of tears, but the grief was more pointed for me, as the image began to meld with the memory of Maisie's death; the snow morphed into concrete, the dog's eyes switched from brown to blue, and I could have sworn I saw the police's red-and-blue lights duly reflected on her fur. Thankfully, I was snapped out of my daze by the revving of a snowmobile and looked over to see Lacie speeding off with the dog—a woman after mine own heart.

Afraid to leave her alone, I commandeered the only remaining snowmobile and made chase, but I didn't have to go far, as Lacie had no fuel and sputtered to a stop within a few feet. I got off near her, expecting to see her crying and steeling myself to comfort her, but I was the one in need of consolation; I broke down, and she held me with one arm and the dog in the other, only crying slightly once the vet had done the deed.

The ground was too frozen for a proper burial and, unwilling to see the dog's corpse lying discarded until the final racers had passed, Lacie insisted on searching the nearest village for an incinerator that could function as a crematory. She didn't want me to go with her, in large part due to Laura's characterization of her abandoning an expensive trip almost at its onset as rude, but I assured her the race had suddenly lost its allure; despite this, she persisted in the belief she'd ruined my vacation and tried to make up for it by coming up with other exciting things for us to do, which in late winter Alaska, as you can imagine, was quite an undertaking.

It was too cold for any extended hikes in the national parks, and the urban attractions, though charming, paled in comparison to what I was used to, but worse than the boredom was the pressure to feign interest lest her consternation be increased, especially since it meant that there was now a degree of phoniness in each meeting; at the end of a particularly long night, as she was listing off potential excursions for the next day, I told her I was feeling a bit sick and that I'd need some rest. She accepted, and to ward off guilt at having unnecessarily worried her, I popped an extra pill before falling asleep; I took some more first thing in the morning, this time to keep thoughts of her at bay, which I knew were crazy when I found myself considering a move to Alaska.

Revolted by that impulse, I thought about calling my travel agency to arrange for an earlier flight; I desisted, however, thinking the urge to flee to be insane, though not in the same way or to the same degree as the impulse to stay forever. The folly lay in the desire to protect her from my using her as an antidepressant and the necessarily resultant obsession. In addition to being an unfairly harsh assessment of myself—with the exception of a fleeting thought that I had no intention to act on, I demonstrated none of the creepiness that defined my relationship with Maisie—as well as being emblematic of the melodramatic and melancholic thinking I was trying to learn to resist, I wrote off the option of simply enjoying her company while it lasted and the memory of it afterward.

I called her, explaining I'd miraculously recovered and that my concierge had provided me with an ample list of potential excursions, if she was still interested in showing me around; in actuality, I had compiled the list myself by perusing the Internet, but I hoped that having another person to attribute it to would, in the likely event that the outings were dull, allow us to heap calumnies on him, guaranteeing at least a modicum of entertainment. It turned out to be an unnecessary precaution, as once the burden of ensuring my enjoyment was lifted from her and that of faking enjoyment was taken from me, I was freed to focus on her conversation, which was enough to put me in such a good mood that even if there were things worthy of complaint, I was couldn't be bothered to take note of them.

Even this, however, I couldn't allow to go unspoiled; I'd remind myself that our growing cordiality was rooted in a major lie of omission, and as the number of skipped opportunities to tell her about my zoophilic nature grew, so did my self-loathing. After a couple of nights, I couldn't hide my agitation well enough for it to go unnoticed by Lacie, and had not my fear of revealing myself been so overweening, I wouldn't have been able to resist her entreaties to unburden myself. In a transient period of sanity, it occurred to me that I didn't know for a fact she'd shun me if she knew the truth; there was a possibility, however slim, that someone would at least try to understand if I could provide a coherent explanation—and who'd be more likely to do so, I thought, than her?

I knew I wouldn't be able tell her the truth in person, since I wasn't confident in my ability to keep from reading into her reactions, and shifting my explanation accordingly, I opted for writing instead, desperate to have something ready to give her before my departure. The days together seemed to provide me with enough of a reservoir of happiness that I could spend almost the entirety of each night writing, and on the night before my flight back, I was able to present her with an envelope that contained what would become the first two chapters of this book and the appended treatise.

Authorship

I realized, to my regret, in the days after the handoff, that since my focus was solely devoted to writing, I didn't consider, and therefore, wasn't prepared for, the anxieties that arose almost immediately after I gave it to her. I wondered if her lack of response meant she hadn't read it, or if she had, and concluding that I was insane, she had simply opted to avoid contact. For once, my tendency to assume the worst was liberating; the objective insanity inherent in sharing a document like this was quite humorous, and I just waited for the cops to knock down my door and arrest me on suspicion of animal abuse.

Most importantly, the prospect of being outed as a zoophile forced me to consider what I had to lose if that did happen, which I realized wouldn't be much; I'd lose a job I hated and friendships, the maintenance of which had grown to be a burden. Not having the opportunity to lie to everyone I'd meet for the rest of my life about this part of me was worrisome, but once I managed to frame it more healthily—that I'd be restricted to open and honest relationships—it almost seemed like a boon; maybe when the headlines screamed, "Man Pens Manifesto

About Poodle Doodling," one of the readers would become my next lover.

This mode of thinking transformed more than my anxiety about Lacie's opinion; it changed the things I centered my life around. If I didn't care about losing this job and it actively stressed me out, then why didn't I quit? Unable to come up with a satisfactory answer, I did just that. If I didn't place any importance on the acceptance of my friends, why were my relations with them predicated on extracting that? I couldn't answer this, either, so I stopped looking to them for it. I still hung out with them, but now our conversations were dominated by talk of their lives, which made our outings more enjoyable for them and me.

My psychiatrist commented on a marked improvement in my demeanor, despite concerns raised by my quitting. I explained to her that I'd ensured I was financially secure, having invested my inheritance so that I could live off dividends—albeit frugally—in perpetuity, but she was unconvinced, stating that work has a more significant role in the lives of twenty-first century Westerners than just as a means of obtaining income. I agreed that I'd have to find something to fill my days, so we compromised, and I began volunteering at a shelter—for homeless people, not animals. Not only was this work fulfilling, but it also gave me the added comfort of knowing that if Lacie decided to expose me and my investments went south, forcing me to live at the shelter myself, I'd at least have made a good impression on my housemates.

I still re-read the writing I'd given to Lacie, but not with the same panic as earlier; when I'd come across an unclear passage, rather than berating myself for my ineloquence and general stupidity, I thought of what I was trying to communicate and how it could be done more efficiently. Soon, my only regret in having shared it with her was doing so prematurely; though I was tempted to send her a revised copy, I decided against it. A few weeks elapsed, enough time for me to wholly dispense with my worries, when after making a call I'd missed, she sent me a text, saying, "We need to talk."

"No, we don't," I fired back, assuming that disapproving of my nature, she wished to lecture me; I managed to keep from demonizing her only by forcing myself to remember that had I not met her when I did, I'd likely have acted on that day's suicidal ideations. She called again and I rejected it, hoping to underscore my unwillingness to speak, but I noticed she'd left a voicemail, and out of curiosity, I decided to listen to it. I couldn't make out much of what she said due to her panicked sobbing, but I gathered it wasn't what I thought, so I called her back.

She explained that although she had read my piece, it was too disjointed and rough for her to know what to make of it, and she hoped that it'd be more intelligible after some copy editing; this meant typing it afresh on her laptop, which she didn't realize her sister Laura, who had moved in with her, would snoop through. Thinking it was written by Lacie, Laura would surreptitiously send herself copies of the document every night, which she would read thoroughly, noting any additions or revisions.

By the time Lacie was ready to send me her feedback, Laura had threatened to out her as a zoophile if she didn't give in to her demands, foremost among which was the transfer of ownership of Lacie's house, which, in Laura's opinion, she had unfairly inherited. Lacie attempted to convince her it was fiction, not autobiographical, but because of her belief that it all *"had to come from somewhere,"* Laura remained implacable. Out of options, Lacie hoped I'd understand she had to out me herself.

My newfound self-acceptance proved to be purely theoretical, and though I was sympathetic, I was so afraid that I offered to buy her a new house once I'd been able to sell my childhood home, which lay abandoned since my institutionalization. She was afraid of seeming impetuous, but since she knew that Laura would have power to sever any relationships she had in Anchorage and would doubtless hold it over her for the rest of her life, she asked if she couldn't just move to the house I'd have sold so as to try and build a new life, promising to pay me rent until she could find a place of her own. I accepted and she thanked me, as if it wasn't a piddling effort on my part to make up for destroying her life.

She bought a ticket for the following week, which was more than enough time for me to remove the evidence of the extent of my obsession—surveillance equipment and the mauled dildo, etc. While taking down the feeds, I noticed that Rana's condo was vacant. My suspicions that, spooked by the break-in, she had returned to her old home was confirmed when, leaving to buy Lacie some toiletries, I ran into her outside; she was going back in to call Chip, who'd moved in with her, when I told her we'd have to catch up later. Thinking that new friends, even ones as uninteresting as these two, might help ease Lacie into her new settings, I told Rana that I had a friend coming that I'd like her and Chip to meet, before calling Quincey's owner to say the same thing to him.

To minimize the difficulty of navigating these social waters, I decided to tell them as much of the truth as possible—Lacie was a friend whom I'd met on vacation, and she needed a place to stay—while leaving out anything about the crisis that necessitated her move. It was an easy topic to avoid because most of our first night together was spent with them opening up to her. I learned more about them while listening to her conversations with them than I had the entire time I'd known them; for instance, Quincey's owner, I found out, had a name: Jordan. These new insights served to soften my view of them, and not only did it mitigate the shame I'd had upon the prospect of introducing them to her as friends of mine, it almost made me look forward to getting to know them further.

Unfortunately, I had more to concern myself with than the formation of meaningful friendships; Laura began demanding ransom payments, and to pay them, I needed to get a job. I couldn't return to my old one—they were no longer under any obligation to take me on since I'd quit—and my inability to get a reference put a damper on my chances of getting a job in the industry; I wasn't bothered by that, as I had no desire to re-enter the field, and given Laura's lack of ambition regarding extortion, I was sure I'd be able to make the necessary payments while working just about any job. Fortunately, the charity I'd been volunteering for was looking to hire a bookkeeper, and I was able to slide into that role.

If you'd told me during business school that I'd be working as a bookkeeper, I'd have probably attacked you for levying what I'd have considered to be a grave insult, but if you'd added to that an assurance that I'd be happier than I'd ever been, I'd have told you that you were crazy; the only downside was that the job necessitated living in the city, away from the suburbs and Lacie. I'd travel back for weekends, which would invariably include a get-together with our increasingly intimate group of friends, and when I was lucky, a little time for us to spend together. With time she'd told me that my insistence on staying in a motel during my trips, though considerate, was unnecessary, and that I could spend those nights at home with her, which I did more often than not in the same bed.

Had it not been for Laura's insatiability, I think my bliss could have lasted forever, but as she'd developed a tolerance for the drugs she'd been using, she demanded more money to fuel her habit. Although I was able to save some money when after a few months, Lacie invited me to move back in, much of the savings on rent were spent on the commute, and my financial situation soon became untenable. The only option, besides murdering Laura—which, despite its elegance as a solution, would prove taxing to my relations with her sister—was to release the writing myself.

Lacie didn't think it prudent, saying that the world wasn't ready for it and that I wasn't prepared for the backlash that would inevitably follow from being publicly labeled "the dog-fucking guy" for the rest of my life—despite the noted absence of any dog fucking—but she helped me nonetheless. I'd dictate to her over the phone while at work, and we'd edit what we came up with at nights. She won from me a concession to use a pseudonym for each person who appeared in it, arguing that my thoughts on Rana, Chip, and Jordan would rupture our friendship with them and cause them unnecessary embarrassment. I pushed back against it, as I thought it'd be cowardly, but I agreed once I began to think her stance was motivated at least in part by being associated with it herself.

It took me a while to realize that my suspicion, as well as the perception of coolness on her part that came with it, was a figment of my deranged mind; the understanding she displayed throughout the writing process, which as you can imagine, was quite emotionally exposing, was all I allowed myself to place importance in. Not once did I feel myself being rejected or scrutinized in a clinical manner. I felt only a growing sense of intimacy, which by the time we'd completed this book, was such that it came as no surprise to her when I asked her to marry me—a proposal she accepted.

Epidogue

Laura, you'll be pleased to find out, died of an overdose shortly after we'd finished writing, rendering the publication of this book—at least from a financial perspective—unnecessary. Lacie thought this meant my zoophilia would remain our secret forever and was baffled when I proposed going wide with it; it was largely due to a justifiable fear that our child, with whom she was pregnant, would suffer if my identity was ever discovered. Although I didn't deny that that would be the case, it was almost impossible to get Lacie to see that it wasn't the most important consideration to make. Our society's stance on zoophilia had to change, but how could it if zoophiles like myself kept themselves muzzled for fear of ostracization?

I knew that although she had something of an understanding of the dysphoria I felt upon the discovery of my zoophilic desires, she never could feel it, and as such, she couldn't fully appreciate the positive impact that reading a book like this might have on a budding zoophile. The thought that one day, after my death, a young man or woman might read this and despite the emotional isolation they'd invariably be feeling, think that they weren't alone after all was lost on her; though nominally a memoir, it could serve as a self-help book for a class of people who could use all the help they can get.

Lacie's reluctance wasn't entirely her fault; her perception of the difficulty in navigating a life when one discovers oneself to be a zoophile was limited. But there were many problems I found myself ill-equipped to discuss with her, like, for instance, the strain it puts on relationships. I couldn't voice my concerns that although she professed to love me in spite of my zoophilia, she wasn't as untroubled by it as she let on.

I first became privy to this when we'd temporarily cared for a rescue dog that her new friends at the local shelter were having trouble finding a home for. Although the dog would sleep at the foot of our bed, I knew Lacie worried that I'd invite it in. It wasn't so much a distrust of me as it was an indoctrinated aversion to zoophiles that created this fear of hers. My bi-speciesism, she assumed, meant that she wasn't enough for me and I wouldn't be fully satisfied unless my zoophilic desires were being met; even if I didn't want to engage in MFD (Male-Female-Dog) three-ways, she thought I'd ask to have, in addition to her, a dog on the side. When we'd have sex, and consumed by passion, I'd close my eyes, I could see upon opening them a look of insecurity in hers that told me she suspected I'd been imagining a dog in her place.

Of course, her discomfort spoke not to a lack of love or a latent disgust toward me; as such, we only required some additional time together for her to be certain of my faithfulness. But if these concerns could be had by a woman as loving as my Lacie, what would be faced by zoophiles who find themselves in relationships with people who aren't as charitable? Would it underscore any sense of disgust they had with themselves and cause an unnecessary resignation to a life bereft of human-human affection? Worse yet, would it not make them feel that they were better off keeping their feelings to themselves, sentencing themselves to an emotional isolation that could lead to feelings of depression and a sense of worthlessness as intense as mine? Having framed it in this way, despite some vestiges of reluctance, she agreed to allow me to publish this as a guide to you, my fellow zoophiles.

To that end, I implore all young zoophiles to resist the urge to conceal this part of yourselves from those whose love you seek and to understand that by lying, you're preventing those who would be tolerant from being able to fully know you, and by extension, to truly love you. Equally important is the need to tell your lover early in the relationship, not only because they'd assume you were lying about your feelings for them and that you were just using them as a beard, but also because it would lessen the pain of a rejection, which given the widespread discrimination we zoophiles face, is a contingency we should prepare ourselves for.

This rush to reveal does not hold true for those of you who came to discover your zoophilia while already in a human-human relationship. Although it may seem like a harsh generalization, it's safe to say that people who are in healthy, fulfilling relationships do not suddenly find themselves lusting after animals, and the very presence of these extra-conjugal, zoophilic desires denotes the existence of fundamental flaws in the relationship you are in; in other words, you should re-evaluate before making what could potentially be a catastrophic admission. Exfiltrating yourself from the relationship and devoting the time that would have been spent lying to soul-searching will leave you better prepared for having the conversation when you find yourself dating someone new.

Once in an accepting human-human relationship, however, you are not out of the woods; any desire to introduce an animal into the bedroom is one that should be fought at all costs. This includes the unlikely scenario in which your partner is aroused by the notion, whether or not they themselves are zoophiles, because of the resultant intellectualization of your sex life together—which, in a healthy relationship, should be, at least for the first few years, purely emotional and passionate; the rapture you should be feeling is not one that will be magnified by the addition of another party, but instead will be suffocated by it—a price not worth the delight and arousal you'll feel during the act.

A partner who rejects your zoo-polyamoristic designs—and therefore, you—is giving you the treatment you deserve, considering the temerity of such a request, and hopefully, a lesson in how to treat the next person you're intimate with; conversely, a partner who would accept it is one who does not have the self-respect necessary to be a healthy life partner, and although you might think you've struck gold, your relationship will surely falter, either when jealousy takes hold or when the insult implicit in being told you aren't enough to satisfy your purported lover becomes too much to endure.

Whether this holds true if your primary bond is with an animal is a trickier determination to make, and it is one that I encourage you to make for yourself. Much of the immorality of infidelity arises from the pain the discovery inflicts on one's partner, and due to the dearth of research on the capacity of animals to experience jealousy, you'll have to gauge the impact any human–human sexual congress might have on them. As a general rule, more possessive animals, like Rottweilers, are not ones that you'd be wise to step out on; whereas, those with more even-keeled lovers, like tortoises, might have more leeway.

Although there may come a time when being a zoophile does not necessitate being an activist, we should not kid ourselves into thinking that time is upon us. Despite my disapproval of human-animal sexual acts, I believe it is imperative that we, the zoophiles of the world, unite to combat anti-bestiality legislation in our states, as such laws cement a hatred of our people within a society—even though, as discussed in my treatise, "On Zoophilia," there is no demonstrable link between the act and love. It is especially important to protest when these laws use definitions of bestiality that are grossly unfair, as is the case in Minnesota, which equates bestiality with necrophilia: "Whoever carnally knows a dead body or an animal or bird is guilty of bestiality."

There is no surer way of leveraging our political power than by coming out as zoophiles. Of course, this might not be possible for some of us, depending on our situations; one should not put the concerns of international zoophilia above their own needs. Although the state of being out is one that is more beneficial to your fellow zoophiles, and by extension, humanity as a whole, being closeted doesn't imply cowardice; it is a natural reaction to the unfair stigma placed upon you by society, a stigma that we all struggle underneath, and which you will eventually learn to bear more effortlessly. It entails difficult conversations, and given the personal costs, your coming out might not be worth the trouble it brings. But I'd implore you to think about the impact your example might have on the trajectory of the life of a zoophilic child of the person with whom you've had it, and recalculate, for we come out not just for ourselves, but for the generations of zoophiles to come. In taking this pain upon ourselves, we are lifting it from them.

To generate enough strength to go public, however, you'll first need to come out to yourself by learning to accept that animals make you horny and that there's nothing inherently wrong with that. This will require both a level of self-awareness that your detractors are incapable of—it is often those who possess a latent, unintellectualized zoophilia that decry it the loudest—and an intellectual honesty dogged enough to enable you to think past the indoctrination you've received, and you should pat yourself on the back on both counts. Though the process might have you feeling down—or as was the case with me, suicidal—going through it will give you a confidence that will be the foundation of a life happier than you thought possible.

Once you're able to do this, which can be as simple as saying out loud to yourself, "I am a zoophile," then you must begin to find those people in your life whom you can confide in first, for there is no need to rush to tell the world just yet. Reach out to a parent, a best friend, or a particularly close sibling—anyone who can help you take this baby step toward self-acceptance. If you lack the confidence for a direct approach, possibly because you're unsure of the person's reaction, I would recommend purchasing a copy of this book for your loved one, as it might serve as a conversation starter. Feel free to insult me and say you only read this book to laugh; I'll forgive the insult so long as you don't simply let them borrow your copy. (On that note, keep in mind that this book would also make a great gift for any prigs in your life whose acquaintanceship you'd like to terminate, as well as all but ensuring the success of any insanity pleas for crimes committed with this book in your possession.)

Finally, to my readers in the near future, think of yourselves not as woebegone and born in an uncaring time, but as a pioneer on the frontier of zoophilia acceptance; we will go down in history as the ones who sacrificed to bring this mode of living into the mainstream, and our pain is a small price to pay for that eternal glory. To my readers born later—when this book is no longer the only romantic novel about an animal, but part of a vibrant sub-genre—to whom our pain will hopefully seem alien, do not honor us by dwelling on the misery of our experiences but by expressing your zoophilia as openly and as happily as we have always wished we could.

On Zoophilia

Though coupled in our minds with lechery, an erection is not necessarily borne from them; it is clear, given my frame of mind when I discovered my first zoophilic erection, that my turgidity was an involuntary response to an innocent emotion—an intimacy boner, so to speak. A detractor might conceivably ask how an erection could be innocent and might even go so far as to say that it speaks to a desire to have sex, whether or not I was cognizant of it, but that is rooted in a misunderstanding of the relationship between affection, or love, and sex: that love is a flowery reframing of libidinous desires. In actuality, lust is not the root of all attraction, and love is not a sublimation of it; lust and love are triggers of separate reproductive strategies, which despite both culminating in boners, are distinct at every preceding point.

Traits that increase an organism's likelihood of passing on its genes, which the stiffening of the penis to facilitate sexual congress does, are often favored in spite of—or before the manifestation of—certain pleiotropic effects. That is to say, A could evolve because of reason B, but could also result in C, D, and E; even if love was initially favored because it functioned as some sort of emotional overdrive switch for horniness, it isn't necessarily the only dynamic at work. Before readily accepting the linear relationship between boner and sex, we must ask ourselves, therefore, if an erection has any causes other than lust.

Although humans can be drawn to sexual displays, like baboons to red buttock pads, or to competitive prowess, like ewes to a gladiatorial ram, we recognize that following lust alone into a relationship opens us up to futures good neither for ourselves or our offspring, and we know this risk is mitigated if we take the time to get to know and bond with the person we're opening up our lives to; this is because we have to navigate psychosocial dynamics, not present in the lives of either the baboons or the sheep, which can bring about situations so stressful that children could not be raised effectively, or in extreme cases, violence, possibly resulting in mariticide and/or filicide. Love, in this context, is the sense that we can invest ourselves in a relationship—the feeling of safety—and could plausibly have evolved to be a secondary trigger for erections.

There would have been no adaptive pressure acting on this trait, however, if it didn't operate separately, and at times, antagonistically to lust. That this antagonism exists is demonstrated by the use of the term *"red flag,"* which with regard to dating, denotes a personality trait, the discovery of which ends any and all romantic interest, but that isn't sufficient to categorize love as a reproductive strategy; to do so, it would have to be shown that it can, in the absence of lust, bring about relationships in which reproduction occurs. I could expound upon this, but one need only speak to couples who weren't attracted initially, yet found themselves bonding and developed perfectly vibrant relationships.

What, you might be asking yourself, does all this have to do with my hard-on for a dog? Although lust is brought on by tangible stimuli—aesthetics, status, etc.—love's reliance on vague emotional states means it can arise in situations wherein reproduction could not possibly result, as I believe was the case with me. In the moments before the discovery of my surgation, I was in a profound state of emotional and intellectual isolation and my innate yearning for any sense of normalcy was strong enough that, once it came, it mattered not that it was from a dog. That a person would be considered disgusting for feeling this and told to shun the cure speaks to the degree to which our society is biased toward zoophilia. This isn't an ingrained aversion, as I will demonstrate, but a vestige of our species' intellectual myopia.

At the heart of this taboo is the mistaken conflation of *zoophilia*, the feeling of attraction, with *bestiality*, the act of having sex with an animal, which as evidenced by the Oxford English Dictionary's decision to use "savagely cruel or depraved behaviour" as the primary definition, is widely condemned. The irony, however, is that though bestiality and zoophilia might be joined in the minds of those new to this subject, they do not, in the majority of cases, occur together; for the most part, the act (bestiality) is divorced of any form of attraction (zoophilia). This means, therefore, that the human is merely using the animal for the stimulation of their genitals, which is vile, but the failure to make this fundamental distinction prevents people from realizing that zoophilia is the ultimate vaccine for bestiality; the affection would prevent the person from doing anything that would harm the animal.

Since in what I will coin Bogdan's Law of Zoophilia, any animal that would not suffer from a sexual act is too large to safely perform a sexual act with, bestiality would never seriously be entertained by any true zoophile. The unfeeling animal fucker, on the other hand, either would not care, or would desist only from fear that injury to or death of the animal might lead to criminal repercussions, and confounding two such disparate groups, I think you'll admit, is quite unfair to the zoophile.

There are those who, unmoved by the benefits of zoophilia, dismiss it as unnatural nonetheless. In examining this statement—asserted axiomatically by people who'd never thought about it, or possibly anything else, at any length and with any depth—we are limited by a paucity of quality research on zoophilia and must touch upon studies of bestiality and its relative rates. We know that instances of bestiality are significantly higher in rural settings than in urban areas, meaning either that urban settings are a closer approximation of the *"natural state"* of humanity, a notion, I think we'll agree, is laughable, or that bestiality is the natural state of human affairs. The weakness of this is further underscored by the seeming ubiquity of cross-species sex and reproduction among animals we wouldn't consider capable of perversion; although the most famous is the mule (a hybrid between a horse and a donkey), there are many others, including the zorse, the liger, the wholphin, and the beefalo.

To make up for the lack of an evidentiary basis to their belief and to reify their preferences as man's default, the homospeciesists often cite religious texts, most frequently the Bible; not only does it allow them to make a positive argument for the superiority of keeping it within the species (particularly the story of Adam and Eve), but there are explicit denunciations of zoophilia for them to reference as well, the most notable of which is Leviticus 20:16, where it is said that, "if a woman approach unto any beast, and lie down thereto, thou shalt kill the woman, and the beast: they shall surely be put to death; their blood shall be upon them." The blatant disregard for the life of the animal in this verse might have put me off the Bible entirely had it not been for the fact that it includes the most famous story of bestiality, that of Jonah and the whale.

Admittedly, the bestiality in this story is not explicit—read literally, the Bible says that Jonah was inside the whale, and it does not reference any sex between the two—however, when one looks at the natural range of sperm whales, the only whales physiologically capable of swallowing a human, one finds they do not appear in the portion of the Mediterranean Sea that Jonah would have embarked upon; since we know that whatever whale he came across was incapable of swallowing him, it follows that the word *"inside"* was used euphemistically.

It isn't just the Abrahamic religions that encourage zoophilia; Eastern religions are no different. The Lakshmana Temple in India contains numerous sculptures and wood carvings depicting human-animal sexual acts. The same holds true for the religions of ancient civilizations, like that of the Greeks, many of whose demigods were products of bestiality. All this brings to mind a quote by Gandhi: "The various religions are like different roads converging on the same point." He's right, and that point appears to be zoophilia.

Centuries of bigotry have had a cumulative effect that will be hard to undo, but one place from which to start is the adoption of a new definition for zoophilia. Beginning with the standard definition for human-human love ("an intense feeling of deep affection"), I suggest only a slight addendum: *"an intense feeling of deep affection toward animals."*

This, unfortunately, would draw the ire of pet owners and self-described animal lovers, who would protest at being lumped in with people like myself; it is clear, therefore, that we must create subdivisions of zoophilia, as is the case with human-human love. The love of a parent for their child is so analogous to that of a pet owner for their pet that many owners refer to themselves as the animal's parents. It seems clear, therefore, that the name for this type of affection should be storgic zoophilia.

But try as I might to provide a description of my zoophilia, the emotions are too raw to be summarized with the coldness necessary for an essay; so, if you allow me, I will close by switching to a form more fitting: the sonnet.

What does my zoophilic love confer?

Tranquillity, on days even most dark

Elation pure each time I stroke her fur

Or hear her richly melodious bark

Yet all that joy can instantly depart

Replaced by fear that makes me bawl and wail

In the intervals between each stop and start

Of the wagging of her downy soft tail

Only the cold of heart can think it sick

This mere indulgence in sweet love divine

Simply because it's sparked by the wet lick

Given to me by Rana's pet canine

So savor shall I each gentle kiss

From fair *Canis lupus familiaris*

Acknowledgements

I've opted to identify the people I'd like to thank in this section only by their initials—since I imagine a good deal of them would prefer not to be publicly associated with this book—but doing so forced me to confront the fact that there is one group whom I can offer no such protections—my family. As such, I'd like to begin with a brief apology to them.

I was born in Somalia shortly before the civil war. There was quite a bit of uncertainty regarding the fate of the country, and my mother was under a lot of pressure to stay and wait things out. Thankfully, she was unable to accept everyone's reassurances and decided to leave, taking me and my older brother—two and five respectively— from Mogadishu to Nairobi and then to Canada. About that trek I know only that it was made in large part on foot, that it was too traumatizing for her to talk about, and that the only thing that got her through it was the determination to ensure for her children the best life possible. It must be quite displeasing, therefore, to know that the life you saved is being used to write a book about a man's love for a dog. To make it up to you, mom, you have my permission to tell any relatives who ask about me that I'm dead.

Although my father has been dead since 2009, the possibility that the publication of this book would cause him anguish in the afterlife has motivated me to make a similar apology to him. I know this wasn't what you had in mind when you taught me to read and write, but I hope you don't regret doing so. I know that the family name meant a lot to you, and I'm sorry for forever tarnishing it. Had I known I'd end up writing a book like this when you died, I would have asked the good people at the cemetery to make your grave wide enough for you to comfortably spin in.

To my five siblings, who can do just about anything for the rest of their lives without being considered the black sheep of the family, I have only this to say: you're welcome.

A very special thanks to my editors—A.J. and T.B.— for their excellent insights. I wouldn't have had the confidence to self-publish if it wasn't for your incredible work. I'd also like both thank and apologize to the freelance editors who decided—upon reviewing my manuscript—that they didn't want to have anything to do with this book. I'm ashamed to admit I derived a great deal of pleasure from imagining you forcing down your disgust long enough to write me a polite note of declination, and I hope that any therapy you sought out after reading this wasn't too expensive.

Throughout the writing process I received a great deal of encouragement and validation from a group of people I'll refer to only as the Rs of the A. Most notable among them is L.Y., whose feedback has done more for me than any anti-anxiety pill ever could, and who, by my calculation, shares at least 27% of the blame for the release of this book. I'd also like to thank J.W., J.D., A.T., R.S., M.H., D.L., P.W., Y.A., and M.R.

Finally, I'd like to thank the people who — although we've only interacted digitally— have had a noticeable impact on the trajectory of my life: P.K., K.S., and B.H. I never allowed myself to seriously consider a career in comedy before receiving your encouragement, and I will always be thankful to you for making writing feel like more than just a pipe dream.

www.ingramcontent.com/pod-product-compliance
Lightning Source LLC
Chambersburg PA
CBHW030934060726
47591CB00005B/1795